# BOYS AND GIRLS SCREAMING

BOYS AND GIRLS SCREAMING

KERN CARTER

DCB

Canadian Heritage / Patrimoine canadien

Canadä

Canada Council for the Arts / Conseil des arts du Canada

ONTARIO CREATES | ONTARIO CRÉATIF

ONTARIO ARTS COUNCIL CONSEIL DES ARTS DE L'ONTARIO an Ontario government agency un organisme du gouvernement de l'Ontario

Ontario

We acknowledge financial support for our publishing activities: the Government of
Canada, through the Canada Book Fund and The Canada Council for the Arts;
the Government of Ontario, through the Ontario Arts Council, Ontario Creates,
and the Ontario Book Publishing Tax Credit. We acknowledge additional funding
provided by the Government of Ontario and the Ontario Arts Council
to address the adverse effects of the novel coronavirus pandemic.

LIBRARY AND ARCHIVES CANADA CATALOGUING IN PUBLICATION

Title: Boys and girls screaming / Kern Carter.
Names: Carter, Kern, author.
Identifiers: Canadiana (print) 20210390883 | Canadiana (ebook) 20210390921 |
ISBN 9781770866454 (softcover) | ISBN 9781770866461 (HTML)
Classification: LCC PS8605.A777825 B69 2022 | DDC JC813/.6—dc23

United States Library of Congress Control Number: 2021951279

Cover art: Nick Craine
Interior text design: Tannice Goddard, tannicegdesigns.ca

MIX
Paper from
responsible sources
FSC® C016245

The interior of this book is printed on 100% post-consumer waste recycled paper.
Printed and bound in Canada.

Manufactured by Friesens in Altona, Manitoba, Canada in February, 2022

DCB Young Readers
AN IMPRINT OF CORMORANT BOOKS INC.
260 SPADINA AVENUE, SUITE 502, TORONTO, ON M5T 2E4
www.dcbyoungreaders.com
www.cormorantbooks.com

*To my daughter, Krystasia.*
*You've inspired a lifetime's worth of stories.*
*I love you more than you can ever know.*
*Thank you.*

# PART I

# CANDACE

## 1.

IT WAS QUIET THAT night. I was only five, sitting cross-legged in the corner of my bedroom with more paint on my arms and legs than there was on the paper in front of me. I could hear her pacing. Every step made its own creak, back and forth like a rusted seesaw.

I don't know what took her so long. It's not like she ever wanted me.

"You shouldn't be here." I must've been three the first time she said those words to me. If I close my eyes tight enough, I can see the black moles dotting her face. Hear the slow, deep crawl of her voice.

"I'm leaving," she said. "You hear me?" She was standing in the doorway of my bedroom holding a gym bag in one hand and a suitcase in the other. I was still holding on to that paintbrush.

There was paint all over my face, on my elbows, and all over my clothes. I looked up at her, but she didn't move any closer. The last sound I remember is the click of the front door lock.

Days later I was still in my room. Still splashing paint and dusting crumbs of dry cereal off sheets of paper covered in blotches of color. That was when I heard the front door. Loud knocks. Then banging. I held my breath and tried staying still.

"Candace? Candace, you in there? We're coming in, OK?"

I shut my bedroom door and hustled to the corner near the window. The paper was still wet with paint when I squeezed it to my chest. Hearing the front door open made me jump back against the wall.

*Go away.*

All I wanted to do was keep painting.

"Candace?" My bedroom door opened. "Candace, are you OK?"

The property manager's face was the first I saw. I only knew him as the man downstairs who said hi every day when I came home from school. Then I saw Mrs. Heard, her hair the same brown as my skin and draped down one shoulder. She took my hand and walked me to the bathroom while the man from downstairs stayed in the bedroom shaking his head.

I had no way of knowing my life was about to change forever. No way to stop Mrs. Heard from cleaning me up and taking me to her home. Ever wasn't in the picture yet, but that first night at Mrs. Heard's house, in my own room with the lights that didn't go all the way dark, I closed my eyes and let myself dream.

And that's exactly what my life became after Mrs. Heard took me in.

She was my kindergarten teacher. After two days of leaving voice messages for my fake mom, she called my property manager and they came to my door. One night went by at Mrs. Heard's, then two. Every morning I woke up thinking my fake mom's face would be the one I saw when I lifted the blanket, but it was Mrs. Heard who tiptoed into my room every morning. I remember one morning after about a week, she tapped my shoulder and asked if I was a little bit hungry or really hungry.

"Really hungry," was my response.

"And do you want bacon with French toast or blueberry pancakes with scrambled eggs or just cereal?"

"Cereal and milk, please."

"Oh yes, can't forget the milk." Mrs. Heard flipped her hair from her shoulder to her back with just the wave of her neck.

"Is my mom coming today?"

"No, sweetie."

"Are you going to send me back to her house?" I hid my face back under the blanket, but Mrs. Heard dipped her head underneath and rubbed her nose all over my cheek before lifting the blanket and cupping my face in her hands.

"My home is your home, Candace."

Their home. My home. My new bedroom was bigger than my fake mom's entire apartment. It had a walkout to a balcony that overlooked the backyard and a bathroom with a silver bathtub that was separate from the shower.

Their home. My home. Mr. Heard said the same thing. He caught me spilling milk on the floor after I tried lifting the box out of the fridge with one hand. I thought I was in trouble. He picked me up from the floor with arms that were almost as pale as the shirt that covered them and told me, "Don't worry, Candace. My home is your home. We're family."

Family. It's a word I'd hear the teachers use at daycare. A word other kids used to talk about their mom and dad.

Here's another word. Mother. A word my fake mother told me never to call her.

"Julia," she said. "That's my name." And like a nice little girl learning to recite the alphabet, that's what I did. Then one day I asked the man downstairs if he had a Julia too.

He nodded and said, "We all have a Julia, princess."

My fake mom apologized and pulled me towards the elevator. When we got upstairs, she told me it was OK to call her mom, but only when we were outside. But sometimes I called her Mom inside and Julia outside. Sometimes I'd go the whole day without saying her name at all.

My new family didn't give a shit about any of that. I called Mrs. Heard, Mrs. Heard, her husband Mr. Heard, and the nanny, Nanny. Mr. Heard called me Candy. Mrs. Heard called me Sweet Candy. Both names brought me back to the days and days that passed without the stove ever turning on. My fake mom had made me eat strawberry pop tarts or raspberry pop tarts, and both were covered in white icing with sprinkles of colorful candy.

"I like Candace," I told them both.

Ever laughs when I tell her that story, even though it's really not supposed to be funny. But that's Ever. She's lying on her bed in the dull pink silk PJs she only wears on weekends. Small twists of her hair show through the yellow and green head-tie wrapped around her curls. She can't help squinting while scrolling through her phone.

I hate that I can't keep my eyes off her, that I've memorized every beauty mark on her face, every group of freckles most people can only see if they get right up close. But I know where to look, know the shapes they make along her cheekbones.

One evening when I'd been living with the Heards for over a year, Mrs. Heard came home, lifted me up in the air and kissed my face, then sat me on the counter beside the sink. Mr. Heard was right beside her. I was in the kitchen rolling meatballs with Nanny. She was in a light blue tracksuit, the same one she wore nearly every day. Her dreads were wrapped loosely to the top of her head and it looked like one good shake would turn them loose. That day was so hot she wouldn't let me go outside, so we'd spent the afternoon baking red velvet cupcakes.

"Something must be tickling your tummy, Clare," Nanny said. "Must be good news."

"Great news," Mrs. Heard replied, then turned to me. "You can stay here forever now, sweetie. You don't ever have to leave."

"Forever?"

"Yes. Forever."

Mrs. Heard's eyes turned shiny like the marble countertop I was sitting on. She was nestled up under Mr. Heard's arm waiting for me to say something.

"Nanny and I made meatballs. They're almost ready so we need to set the table."

Mrs. Heard laughed so loud she snorted. I raised my arms so Mr. Heard could lift me off the counter. I hopped over to the drawers and took out three forks. Nanny had already set out the plates so I just put the forks beside each one then opened the fridge and grabbed the box of lemonade with both hands.

"Mrs. Heard?"

"Yes, sweetie."

"I don't wanna call you Mrs. Heard anymore."

"That's fine, sweetie. What do you want to call me?"

"Mommy."

My new mother put her hand to her mouth and turned away. I looked at Mr. Heard to see if I said something wrong but he was smiling so I knew I was good. A week later I asked if I could call him Daddy.

Just like that, I became a Heard. No one from my fake mom's family had a problem with the Heards adopting me. Most of them had never even met me, but I didn't care. The only stories I'd heard about my fake mom's family were about her mother. Like the day when one of my fake mom's younger sisters found their mother lifeless on the couch with a cigarette dangling from her mouth and the TV turned on. When my fake mom got home, both her sisters were sitting on their mom's lap staring at the screen. Sounds messed up, but from the other stories I heard, they were probably better off. Two rooms, three children, and a mother who was out more than she was in. When she was in, my fake mom said the house trembled.

When I think about it, I did have something in common with my fake mom: we both had mothers who resented us. For her, forgetting to put the cap back on the toothpaste meant a slap to the face. Complaining about a meal meant they didn't eat that night. A messy room meant the belt.

My fake mom didn't get down like that. She never once hit me or even threatened to, and she hardly ever raised her voice. She'd sit and read Romantic poets while I searched through the fridge or climbed up on the counter to look for cookies or cereal in the cupboards. I'd hear the pages flip and try to keep my balance, jumping down only when I found something to keep my stomach from making those sounds.

Once when I couldn't get down from the counter, she just watched me. Wordsworth or Coleridge weren't enough anymore, but seeing me struggle to find a way to safely make it down without losing whatever snack I'd picked up to stop the grumbling kept her attention.

"You better not," my fake mom said. It was the first time I fell off the counter and she saw me getting ready to cry.

"That won't be necessary," she said. Like she was buying a new pair of jeans and one of the staff asked if she'd like to try them on. Won't be necessary. Like she'd just finished dinner at a restaurant and the server asked if she'd like to see the dessert menu. She stared at me while my chest pumped and deflated. The cereal box was crushed on the floor in front of me, but I don't remember feeling any pain.

"Get up and take that box to your room."

When I didn't move, she grabbed the box and my hand and pulled me to my room and shut the door.

Creak.

Creak.

She walked back to the couch and turned another page.


2.

IT WOULD BE WRONG to call me and Ever friends because we never were. We were sisters from the first day we sat beside each other on the floor for storytime. By the end of that day, I handed her my paintbrush, the one I'd kept from my old life. She grabbed my hand and painted *Ever*. When I told her I didn't know how to write my name, she spelled it out on the back of her right hand.

"See," she said. "It's easy."

Wasn't long before I learned how to paint my own name on her hand. I did it so much you could see faded letters where I'd written the day before. We talked too much. That was what Mrs. Leach said every time she had to call us from the corner of the classroom where all the backpacks hung from two rows of short hooks. We thought the bags kept us hidden, but Mrs. Leach always found us and forced us to join the other first graders grouped in front of her.

I remember showing my mom Ever's name on my hand and telling her we were sisters. Once our parents realized we were only one park away from each other, we ended up at each other's house every weekend. Then every weekend turned into every other day.

That meant telling Ever everything. My fake mom was only a story by then. Someone I knew was real, but spoke about like she was a character I painted. When I told Ever about how she left me it felt like I was in my room again. Not alone this time, though.

"You lived in an apartment?" Ever asked. We were in my room lying on our bellies, not paying much attention to the dolls in front of us.

"Yeah, on the fourteenth floor. Sometimes the elevator didn't work and we had to walk up the stairs."

"All the way up to fourteen?"

"Yup, and back down again too."

Ever's eyes were wide. "Were you surprised when she left?"

I tried untangling my doll's hair. Ever took my being distracted as me not wanting to answer.

"My mommy would never do that," she said.

"My new mom says she'll never do that to me, either. She says my fake mom was sick."

That's how we talked. Ever throwing questions at me and me answering no matter what. Piano lessons, weekend swimming lessons, and skiing on winter weekends kept us busy together. The travel back and forth was always the most fun, me and Ever in the back seat singing songs we'd learned in school, mumbling through parts we couldn't remember.

I always secretly hoped we would end up back at Ever's place. Not only because they had a chef who let us in the kitchen and slipped us shrimp without the tails, or let us pile up all the crumbs from one of his cakes and pour icing all over it before stuffing our faces. It was really because of Jericho.

There was something about Ever's younger brother that made me want to sit beside him and share my toys. He was never really interested. He'd indulge me for a few seconds before taking his building blocks and moving them somewhere else, away from me. It didn't matter, though. Sometimes I followed him around before Ever reminded me that I'm her friend, not his.

But when Ever came by my house one Saturday afternoon and brought Jericho with her, I couldn't help but share my paintbrush. It was impossible not to tell him how well he drew clouds and trees, and when he mixed green and red and purple to make this nasty looking color, I still used it on my pictures. Only Nanny was home with us that day. We were in the hallway outside my room with large sheets of plain paper covering the floor. Ever asked me to go get more paint from my room, and while I shuffled through my art box, I heard footsteps creeping towards me. I turned around and was relieved to see Jericho standing with his head down. We were both facing each other, but he couldn't look at me.

My mind took me back to the time when I stood outside my fake mother's room and listened. That time I peeked because the hanger she put on top of the door to dry her towel meant it never closed all the way.

"Jericho!" Ever was standing under the arch of my room door with a tube of empty paint in her hand. "Leave Candace alone." Ever looked at Jericho the same way she does today when she's ready to pounce. "You're not playing with us anymore? Go play by yourself."

Ever grabbed Jericho's hand, marched him out of my room and put him in a corner away from us.

"What's going on up there?" Nanny's voice was stern enough to scare other kids. She scared me the first few times we spent the day together, but her voice quickly became reassuring. She could make me feel safe with just a few words.

"Nothing, Nanny," and maybe I meant it. But that memory of my fake mother made me want to stay in my room by myself and shut the door. I was too young to recognize I was still healing, but still very aware that Ever was there with me. Something in her made us stop painting and she gave me a hug. How tiny we must have been back then. We looked like two dolls embracing in the middle of my bedroom.

Nanny had made her way upstairs by then and smiled when she saw us hugging. Jericho was still squirting paint aimlessly on the paper in front of him. This was my life.

## 3.

I WAS TEN WHEN I learned to ride horses. There was nothing in the world my dad loved more than riding. We'd spend part of the Christmas break plus a few weeks during the summer near a ranch in northern Florida where my dad owned a few horses. Mom watched us from off to the side in sundresses she had made for no other reason, but never once climbed on a horse.

By the time I was thirteen, Dad started calling me an equestrian. That was pushing it. I think he just liked seeing me walk out in full gear.

"Nope, you know the drill, Candace."

We were standing at the side of the field at our Florida ranch. I was nearly in full uniform ready to put my helmet on when Dad stopped me.

"Daddy, I've done this a million times."

"Well this is a million and one times and I'm still going to buckle up your helmet."

That was his excuse to steal a quick forehead kiss. To help me mount my horse and watch my first few gallops before setting his own saddle. Usually, he'd let me ride a little bit ahead, enough so I felt like I was riding on my own but never far enough where a few strides wouldn't put him back next to me.

He had convinced himself that one day he'd see me prancing beside a shiny black horse, preparing to leap on its back while it trotted around in circles.

"No way, Daddy."

That had been my reaction since the first time I saw a girl mount a moving horse. She stood on its back with her arms in the air before somersaulting backwards into a handstand she held for what had to be at least five seconds. "I can't do that."

"You sure?" We were riding side by side by then. "A little practice and you'll be competing in no time."

My dad was a bit clueless sometimes, that was the word my mom used the most, so maybe he didn't get that riding was fun and all, but that was it. Turning it into some kind of competition would change the reason I loved riding so much in the first place, and that was spending time with him.

"Yes, Daddy. I'm sure."

He put on his saddest face and blew me a kiss before letting me pull ahead again.

Being Vice President of the largest bank in Canada, my dad had to make our time together count. We knew when we'd be on vacation, what weekends during the summer we'd stay at the cottage, how long we'd get to ride in Florida before he had to hop back on his jet and avert another crisis. The rigidness of our schedule never bothered me. It actually made me more excited because I'd get to count the days before our next adventure together, the same way I'd get excited when I knew my dad was coming home.

"You awake, sweetie?" That was Dad at two in the morning during the summer after one of his week-long work trips. I'd been waiting to hear his car pull up in the driveway before sliding back under my blanket and pretending to be asleep. His shoes hitting the staircase sounded like we were back at the stables in Florida walking one of the horses. I waited till he stopped outside my room. He tapped me on the shoulder and I turned around as slowly as I could manage, even though it took everything in me not to jump off my bed.

"Looks like somebody can't sleep. What say we sneak downstairs for some hot chocolate?"

I climbed on my dad's back and he carried me down to the kitchen. Our cups were already out, decorated with the first letter of our names. Two sips and my eyelids felt heavy, so I slid off the barstool and leaned up beside my dad, who was still sitting. He knew all I wanted to hear about was his airplane ride home. How long he was in the air. Was it Rob or Angelo who piloted the flight? Was it smooth or did the plane shake?

I fell back asleep before getting most of these questions out and dove deep into a night of wild dreams. Only one dream, actually. The same dream I had over and over. That couch squeaking. Her standing over my crib watching me cry. I dreamt the scent of my old apartment; weed smoke mixed with bleach. My fake mom was singing her favorite song while rubbing baby lotion together in her hands.

> *Sun in the sky you know how I feel.*
> *Breeze drifting on by you know how I feel.*
> *It's a new dawn it's a new day. It's a new life for me.*

She weaved her fingers through my toes to the melody, moisturizing the creases. She raised my head and used her two fingers to lotion my neck. She rubbed both ears at the same time and sometimes, just sometimes, my fake mother let a smile betray her.

I don't even know why I still think of this stuff. It's like it's coded into my DNA and ripping it out means I'd be tearing part of myself out with it. I want to forget her. I really do. Funny how naive I was back then.

Things changed going into eleventh grade. It was a cool evening nearing the end of summer and Ever and I were sitting on her front porch with her mother. Her mom had just cut her own hair almost into a bob with bangs she couldn't stop running her fingers through.

"If you get any darker people are gonna think you gave birth to me," I told her.

"Oh, stop it, Candace. My skin just loves the sun. Plus, you know my mom is as dark as you are so it's in my blood."

Ever's mom smiled with all of her teeth, and when you really got her to belly laugh, she'd close her eyes and tilt her body back with her hand covering her stomach.

The late summer breeze meant we were both wearing oversized sweaters, Ever with jeans and me with cut-offs. Water for us, white wine for Cy. When I first started coming around, it was Mrs. Andrews, then it was Cynthia, then one day she saw me and Ever in the mirror doing our hair. She sat us both down, took the brush and put my hair up in a bun that made me feel like Lauren London. When she was done, I said, "Aaww, sigh." She liked it, so it stuck.

Ever was scrolling through her IG feed and stopping every few minutes to add to her story.

#sisters. #besties. #Longhairdontcare. #Girlsonly.

Making an appearance on Ever's IG was cool because she had a bunch of followers. I mean, like, thousands. She wanted that blue ribbon before we got to high school.

"They should give it to me right now. Like, what do they even base it on?"

"Followers."

Ever pretended to throw her water at me and I shielded myself. "Seriously," she said. "Who do I have to bribe to get that thing? Is there, like, a blue-ribbon group that sits around adding blue ribbons to people's Insta? I need to know."

"Like you would ever message them even if there was."

Cy shakes her head and we all laugh. "God forbid," she said. "We know Ever's favourite saying."

Like a girl group reunited, we said it in unison: *If you're working too hard, there's no point.*

Cy raised her glass and tapped our cups.

"Life can be so easy," Ever said. I hated when I didn't really agree with Ever but still thought she was right.

"So working hard is not a thing?"

"Working hard is too much of a thing. Teachers work all day then go home and grade papers. They do that for, like, fifty years, but then what do they have to show for it?"

"You realize my mom is a teacher, right? There are people out there who like what they do."

Ever rested her cup back down on the small, round glass table Cy had bought at a yard sale that spring.

"Maybe. But no one likes struggling. And your mom definitely isn't struggling."

"How do you know?" I said playfully.

"I know everything, Candace. You should know that by now."

Trying to figure out how Ever thought was like one of those weird social experiments that lasted for decades. She kept scrolling and doubled clicked a few times before Cy jumped in again.

"That's it. Girls, we're going for a drive."

No complaints from either of us. We went straight from the

porch to the SUV, both of us buckled in the back seat. Cy lowered all the windows and turned up the music. Gwen Stefani, Tupac, Nirvana, Tribe Called Quest. She sang along to all of it. We'd heard these songs in the back of her car enough times to mouth some of the words.

Then "Hollaback Girl" came on and it was an all-out concert. Ever and I had our heads out the window screaming the chorus. We waited for Cy to jump in and sing the part we'd never sing in front of her: "*That's my shit, that's my shit.*"

Ever cheered, I applauded. "Mom, you definitely missed your calling. You could've been rich and famous."

"I'll settle for being rich. Less stress."

Last time Cy took us for a drive we ended up at a festival in Stratford. The time before that, we hit the beach in Innisfil. Once we drove somewhere close to Niagara Falls and stayed overnight. She let us sip wine that evening. We never packed any clothes or anything like that, so we shopped half the day and got a bunch of new stuff.

"Where we going this time, Cy?"

"Still figuring it out. Sit back and enjoy. This feels like it might be a long one."

"My dad told me there's a food festival in Woodbridge," I said.

"Girls, girls. Not knowing is the best part. Just put your sunglasses on and let's see where the evening takes us."

We were on the highway letting the wind cool our faces when Cy's phone rang. She looked at the number then put it back down. It rang again and she did the same thing. When it rang one more time, she put it on speaker.

"There better be a good reason for you bugging us, mother."

THERE'S SOMETHING FRIGHTENING ABOUT hospitals. No matter who you look at sitting on the seats or waiting impatiently at the nurse's desk, you know something's wrong. Maybe it's a scrape on the knee, maybe someone tried to clean grass from the bottom of the lawnmower and cut off half their finger. Either way, something's wrong.

What I remember most about that day was quiet. The way we fell quiet in the car as Cy turned us around and sped through side streets to the emergency room. The way Ever and I, and Jericho, who'd come with his grandparents, sat saying nothing in the waiting room.

Ever's silence in particular. It was like watching her scream with no sound. She wasn't sad, she was pissed. Mad at the world for doing this to her father. In Ever's world, bad things weren't supposed to happen. It's another one of her rules. The universe had let her down.

Right before my parents came to pick me up, we were allowed into Mr. Andrews' room.

"He's awake and doing OK for now," the doctor told us. "The heart attack was severe but he got here in time for us to get him somewhat stable."

"Can we see him now?" Cy was wiping her nose with Kleenex when she asked. Her eyes were red and weak and even asking that one question seemed to suck away more of her energy.

"We'll have to operate, but you can see him for a few minutes. Then he has to rest. Family only."

No one even blinked when I got up and walked in. Ever stopped outside the door and reached for my hand. Still no sound. I wrapped my arms around her and we stayed that way while the rest of the family filed past us.

"I love you so much, Candace. I don't know what I'd do without you."

I squeezed tighter and felt her tears on my neck.

"It's not fair," Ever said.

Inside, Cy was sitting on the bed holding her husband's hand. Her parents were standing behind her with Jericho. Her mother looked hopeful even though she didn't say much and Cy's father didn't take his eyes off of Mr. Andrews. He stared and narrowed his bushy eyebrows till it looked like he was squinting. He had as much hair on his arm as he did anywhere else, and I thought he resembled a grizzly bear watching over his cub. Ever went to stand beside Cy and touched her dad's face. The tubes in his nose frightened me. It was hard to remember what he had looked like just hours before.

He could barely speak. "I'm coming home." Those words stretched across the room.

"Of course you are. There is no home without you." Cy kissed her husband on the forehead one more time before the doctor instructed us to let him rest. Ever lingered. I turned around to see her still standing beside her dad. The doctor looked at me and I walked over to Ever.

"Promise me this isn't the last time I'll see you, Dad," she said.

He opened his eyes. I could see her searching his face for some kind of hope. But she knew.

SHE ASKED ME TO sleep over the night before the funeral. We stayed in her room the entire time, scrolling through pictures of us on her phone.

"I can't believe we were so little." Ever seemed genuinely surprised. "Like, when did all this happen? How did we get here?"

"I don't know."

"What's the point?"

The way I looked at Ever must've made her realize what she'd said.

"I just mean ... my dad is gone. We're never gonna see him again." We were sitting on the floor in front of Ever's bed, her head on my lap with tears dampening my pyjama pants.

"I don't get it, Candace. Why my dad?"

"I don't know, Ever. It's just really messed up. Everything."

We finally wore ourselves out and fell asleep side by side on the floor. The last thing I saw was the view through Ever's window. Evergreens that looked like ancient pillars towering over groups of yellow and blue flowers illuminated by perfectly spaced log lights. Herb bushes and plants with leaves big enough to sit on.

THE FUNERAL WAS ON a humid September afternoon that made your neck moist as soon as you stepped outside. No breeze, no relief from the heat that only got worse as the procession continued. Sweat beaded up under our dresses. The sun was covered by darkening clouds we all hoped would end our suffering, but it just got hotter. I didn't know most of the people there. Even when they removed their sunglasses, only a few looked a bit familiar. Friends I'd seen at one of Cy's parties, family that popped by once in a while and knew me as Ever's best friend.

Cy stayed close to her parents. Jericho shadowed Cy's every move. Ever wouldn't let me go.

I let her hold my arm. I let her lean on my shoulder and cry in my lap the entire ride back home. Her home, which felt just as much like my home. We shut ourselves in her room for hours before Cy opened the door and sat on the bed without a word. Her eyes were swollen. She would have been crying, but there was nothing left.

# JERICHO

## 1.

MOM'S LETTER. THAT'S WHERE it all starts.

> To my unborn child,
>
> I can't believe you are actually happening. For so long,
> I didn't know you were possible. I didn't want you to be
> possible.
> Now you're here, kicking and twisting and fighting to come
> into the world. Tears fill my eyes every day. Tears of joy, of
> pain, of fear, all moments I will remember forever and ever.

The story goes that my mother wrote that note because her pregnancy with Ever had been so difficult. On more than one occasion, she had to be hospitalized. The note was my mother's attempt at staying positive and grateful. And she didn't want to forget so she named her Ever. Her first. Her forever. I mean, how do you compete with that?

People always assume they know the significance of my name. Jericho, an ancient biblical city that fell to the Israelites after their army had destroyed the walls of the city by blowing their trumpets. That's way too surface for my mom. It's said that the story of the Good Samaritan took place between Jerusalem and Jericho. My mother would never think of naming me Jerusalem.

"Names are important," she said. "They guide our character. I wanted you to have a kind heart."

My sister's name pointed to an endless existence while mine depicted a historic past. In our names alone, my mother created her own epic.

But how could she have known? How could she have really known how our lives would play out? She didn't even know what would happen at leadership camp. That three other boys and I, a full year into high school, hardly rebellious but more inspired to steal together than any of us ever would've been on our own, would do just that.

Dressed in our darkest shorts and sweaters, we snuck out at night and followed the lampposts through the sand into the closest town. Watching *Mission Impossible* the night before was all the motivation we needed.

My mother had sent me to the camp to be a better leader and here I was leading a team of agents into an unknown town. Mission impossible without the impossible.

"What do you want to do today?" That's how this camp thing started. School had been out for a week and every day my mother asked me questions. "Why don't you give James a call and see what he's up to?" Or, "Why don't you invite Mikey up to the cottage with us this weekend?"

The sight of me sitting idly in my room watching YouTube videos about the Grey Ghost on my iPad for the entire day frightened her. She wasn't someone who planned out our full summers like our other friends. We took family trips to the cottage and vacations to the islands, but those things happened all throughout the year. Mom usually let us figure out our own time over the summer, but that summer she just wasn't having it.

"It wouldn't be the worst thing in the world if you went out and caused a little trouble with your friends."

That was her last attempt. I'm sure she figured if a free pass to be delinquent didn't get me out of the house, she better plan something herself. When we drove to Muskoka that weekend, her boating buddy Angelique told her about the leadership class that her son Adam was signed up for.

"It's only about twenty minutes away, but it's a week where they're outside the house and off their phones." Angelique's sunglasses covered most of her face. She had made her way over to our cottage late that morning and she and my mom were sitting on the front porch drinking some kind of strawberry wine mix. I was standing just outside the front door. "Plus, it's far enough away that they won't just walk back home if they hate it, but close enough that we don't have to be worried about them."

And so there I was, day three of this camp that's supposed to teach me lessons on confidence and how to get people to follow my lead, and I've taken the opportunity to gather a band of curious minds and lead them out of the cabins and into the town. Maybe my mother would be impressed. Maybe, but she would never find out.

It was me, Adam, and two other boys named Michael and Ishan. The night of our adventure, we congregated in my room. Adam was already in my cabin and Michael and Ishan were split into the other two. We sat in a tight circle joining our cell phones together, continually clicking the side button for light. Goosebumps reloaded.

We whispered our secret strategy:

*Don't eat too much at dinner because it might make us tired.*

*Wear our darkest colors. Blues and grays and OK Ishan you can wear red, but at least try to find some dark shorts.*

*Don't put your shoes on till you get outside.*

*Curfew is ten, lights off at eleven, we'll meet at twelve under the first lamp post to the west. That means we have to come out of the front door of our cabins and turn left.*

*Phones on silent till we meet up.*

*We wait till everyone gets there before we leave or we don't leave at all.*

Perfect! And everything did go perfect on the walk into town, which was just as silent as the cabins we'd left. That realization dimmed our excitement. The thrill was over and now we were walking aimlessly through a town with nothing happening and no one to share our escape.

Our collective disappointment led us inside an unlocked café. It had a sliding door that hadn't been closed and we saw this as our last chance for any kind of adventure. We walked in and stood on the small, wooden tables that lined the walls, swung on the barstools and pretended to be dizzy, and played who could throw leftovers the furthest. It was digging in the back kitchen for more food that

Adam saw it sitting beside a short bucket of flour. A jar full of bills and change. He held the jar out in front of him with both hands like a baby that just shit herself and rested it on the bar table.

"Holy shit." Ishan.

"Let's count it." Adam.

"Let's just take it and count it back at our rooms." Michael.

I took Adam's side and $533.25 later, we were talking in mob style accents about splits. Each of us took a turn counting it. I knew the split was $133 each in my head, but still did the math on my phone's calculator. A hundred dollars in the hands of this group of fourteen and fifteen-year-olds wasn't a new experience for any of us, but we still played it up as if this wasn't less than our parents would spend on our knapsacks come back to school.

"How much does *Call of Duty* cost?" was Adam's first question.

"I'm gonna be responsible and save it, said no teenager ever." Michael always tried to be the comedian.

"Where we gonna hide this? My roommates are shady." Ishan trusted two people in this world and one of them was himself.

It took us a few seconds to notice the flashing lights flickering from outside. It took even less time for everyone to run out of the backdoor, money still in their hands, and disappear into the night.

I should've run too. I leapt to my feet, but they wouldn't move.

*Run, Jericho. Move your feet you fucking idiot, those are cops outside. This is not a drill. I repeat, this is not a drill.*

I tried. I really did. But something forced me back down on that barstool and I stopped fighting it. When the police came and saw me sitting there with a wad of cash in my hand and an empty jar marked 'we believe in change' in black and red permanent marker, they cuffed me and put me in the back of the squad car.

Handcuffs are tight. And uncomfortable. And sitting in the back of a cop car incites the kind of fear you get from watching a horror movie when you know something is behind the person and you're hoping they don't turn around. My throat felt dry. The cuffs dug deeper into my wrists every time I shifted positions. When the cop opened his door and sat behind the steering wheel, I thought about what it would feel like walking through the prison yard trying to put on my best gangster face.

"What were you guys doing in there?" I thought it was strange that a cop was wearing glasses. Didn't you have to have perfect vision to be a police officer? And why was he grinning? It was his smile that frightened me more than anything.

So I told that cop everything. From the way we planned our escape up till me sitting in the back of this car. He told me we set off an alarm as soon as we stepped into the cafe. Secret agents should've known that. Either way, I was ready for my punishment.

"Get the money back."

"Huh?"

Mr. Law and Order was peering at me through his front mirror now.

"Get the money back from your friends and we'll forget any of this ever happened."

"Umm, OK, so I'm not going to jail?" I crossed my fingers behind my back even though they were already getting numb.

"Not if you get the money back."

The officer dropped me back at the camp and waited. Less than five minutes later, I came back out with all the money. Before he pulled away, the officer asked me the same question that was running through my mind.

"Why didn't you run?"

The lights on top of the cop car were off. He was leaning against the trunk counting the money when I tried to find an answer.

"I don't know."

He pulled off with the same look Ever gives me when I say something ridiculous. But it didn't make sense to me either. How could my body disobey my mind? Is that even possible? Maybe Mom was right. Maybe my name stops me from doing anything gravely wrong. Maybe I'm the Samaritan. The Good Samaritan who sneaks out of camp and steals money out of someone's tip jar but doesn't run.

When camp was over that week and I was back at my family's cottage, I couldn't resist telling Ever what had happened. For her, there was no mystery.

"You're just a pussy, Jericho."

"Poetic. How ever does Ever do that?"

She hates when I do that, but it's too easy. It's the one thing I can do to get under her skin. Nothing else even comes close to provoking an angry stare or a slap across my back. Plus, it's usually me on the other end of some sideways experiment thing that Ever dreamt up. But Ever doesn't dream. That's what she tells me. All of her imagination is saved for when she's awake. I tell her she's lying. That none of that could be true. Everyone dreams. Everyone. But she told me that people who dream when they sleep are broke. They can't even afford refrigerators that dispense filtered water or won't ever go on a family vacation outside of the country.

These are tragedies, Ever says. Tragedies. Because God knows tap water is disgusting and travelling to a different continent four times a year should be everyone's right. Standard shit. What would Mom say? Funny that I went there, but that was only because I already knew what Dad would say if he heard Ever talking like this. He was still alive then, still teaching us lessons we weren't ready to learn.

"Everything outside of life itself is a luxury." His words. Not his final words, but those are bits of my final memories. I wish I knew that my time with him was coming to an end. Sometimes I sit in my room in the morning and I talk to him. I whisper thoughts and can feel him listening and sense him talking back. Sometimes I swear I can hear him laughing and that makes me laugh too. Quiet enough so I don't wake anyone or for them not to think I'm losing my mind.

But we're not there yet.

It was still summertime. Leadership camp was over, I was feeling good, and who fucking cares. Ever would be so proud to hear me say that. We were still in Muskoka. Adam's parents were having a pool party and we were all crowded up in his backyard. His two cousins were there, which meant his aunt Michelle was there with her husband Jamie. Ever and my mom were also there, and Candace too.

Adam's pool was pretty cool. It wasn't like those all-inclusive resort pools that only go up to four feet. This was the real deal with a deep end that kept parents on guard. I was floating around making my way to the shallow end when I noticed Ever and Candace sneaking off. I caught Ever's eye and she motioned for me to follow.

We huddled by the trees, away from the beach and the weekend cottagers, out of sight of the pool.

"I've never seen this path before," I said.

Ever said she went there every night. The joint was already dangling from her mouth. Candace wasn't paying any attention to us. She was staring at the beach and waiting her turn to hit the joint again.

I was skipped over twice already. Expected, since I'd never smoked anything in my life.

Then Ever said, "You should try this, Jericho. Swimming while you're high is like dreaming with your eyes open."

"I never understand what you mean."

"Who cares," Candace chimed in. "You don't have to understand, all you have to do is inhale."

Puff. Exhale. Puff. Exhale. Puff. Don't cough. Don't do it. Candace's lips.

High as a pilot, or is it a kite? Too high to tell because then I was floating in the pool. Ever was watching me. Hawkeye.

"Go under." I squinted and saw her mouth the words again.

"Go under."

How deep can I go? Can I hold my breath long enough to touch the bottom? Of course I can. Except where's the bottom? I'm upside down and bubbles are coming out of my mouth. Don't breathe, Jericho, that's not air. There's no air. Ever!

## 2.

THE OFFICIAL STORY WAS that my leg cramped and I couldn't swim back to the top. I don't even know where that lie came from or how I knew to make it up. I didn't want my mom knowing I was too high to swim and definitely didn't want my friends to know. Then there was Ever.

I felt her eyes on me the entire time I was under, gasping for air. She didn't say a word to anyone when a minute passed. Two minutes. How many minutes, Ever?

It wasn't easy looking at her in the hospital room. It wasn't easy to watch as she feigned a sense of relief. But I was alive. I don't remember much of what happened. Not how I got out of the pool, how I got to the hospital, nothing.

I woke up in this hospital to the sound of my mother deep breathing on one of those cold, maroon-colored chairs.

An hour later it was just me and Ever in the room. She was sitting on the same maroon seat.

"What are you feeling right now?"

"I was drowning," I said. "You told me to go under."

"What are you talking about?"

"I saw your lips move. You said it twice. It's why I went into the deep end."

Ever pulled on her ear the way she did when she had to think about something for longer than a second.

"Jericho, I don't know what the fuck you're talking about. You were high. You dove into the water and Adam's mom pulled you out. Nothing else happened."

"That's your story?"

"It's not a story. That's what happened."

I wasn't giving up. "I saw you, Ever. I saw you right before I went under. I even saw you while I was under."

"While you were under? Are you listening to yourself? Just ... Jericho, you almost drowned. Get some rest. You're like a plant in the desert right now."

"I don't know what that means."

"Of course you don't. What matters is that you're OK."

Really? Because telling me to do something that was dangerous enough to land me in the hospital seemed pretty important to me.

I wondered what Candace was thinking. I wondered how she felt about all this. I don't remember seeing her at the hospital, but I'm sure she remembered exactly what happened. I was allowed back home the same day and headed straight for the jacuzzi in our backyard when she popped up with my sister.

"How excited are you right now?" Ever said.

Ever sure knew how to make an entrance, but she was right. Every time I saw Candace, my forehead got hot and I got this feeling in my chest like I was at the top of a roller coaster about to make its first big drop. Before Candace got into the hot tub, she took her time taking off her towel. I watched her fold it carelessly and drop it on the ledge. Seeing nearly all of her skin somehow glow in the shade of the early evening made me thankful most of my body was submerged.

When Candace sat in the hot tub after Ever, her body was all I could think about. She got so close to me I could see each droplet on her neck sliding down her shoulders and dripping into the water. We side-glanced each other. Sometimes she'd stare straight at me and I'd shift my eyes to any other part of her body so I didn't give my thoughts away. I was also pretty sure she kissed me that day we all smoked. It's not one of those memories I'm willing to bet on, but it's something I see in my mind.

She knew all of this. Her movements were too calculated. It was why I kept all my thoughts of her sealed in my mind. Part of me knew she was just fucking with me. She was Ever's friend and I never forgot that. I could never take anything she did at face value. The moment I even thought to act on any of these signals was the minute they'd both make me wish I'd drowned for real.

"What did you mean you saw me while you were under?" Ever said.

Time and place, I think. It was what Mom would say.

"I don't know. Maybe it was whatever drugs they had me hooked up to —"

"Or maybe you meant what you said."

"Maybe."

"Oh, I get it. This is my punishment for giving you your first puff of weed. You're just not gonna answer any questions?"

"I already gave you an answer. You told me I don't know what I'm talking about so why are you asking me now?"

"Well look what we have here. Little Jericho finally growing some balls. OK, what do you want? An apology? Sorry I made you try a little weed. Sorry I made you get in the pool. Sorry I figured you can actually fucking swim."

"Be nice, Ever," Candace said.

"He got his apology."

*One day closer to forever.*

Ever had tatted that on her forearm in grade nine. How she got someone to do it despite her being only fourteen wasn't even a question my mother wasted her time with. Instead, she asked her why those words were inspirational enough to tattoo on her body. Ever said it was her fortune and that was good enough for my mother.

Sometimes Dad and I would just sit on the couch and watch Ever and my mother lying on their backs with their shoulders touching for hours. They weren't sleeping. Sometimes Ever would roll over on her stomach and Mom would let her rest her head on her shoulder before they were back to being on their backs. It was like this strange ritual, unrehearsed, but very much in sync.

Ever didn't say anything else to me the rest of the time we were in the hot tub. She put her head back and zoned out for a bit, then just got out of the tub, grabbed her towel and left the backyard.

"Ever," Candace said to me. "Gotta love her, right?"

"You must. You've been her friend since before I could speak in full sentences."

"I don't know exactly what it's like to be her brother, but it's easy to be her friend."

"If you say so."

"I do say so."

Forehead heat.

"You know what else I think?"

Funny feeling in my gut.

"I think we're alone."

Don't fall for it, Jericho. Do not fall for it.

"Alone, half-naked, hot, and wet ..."

No way this was fucking happening. She's fucking with me.

"Put your hand right here. Feel that." Oh my God. "Do you feel it?"

"Yes."

"I'm gonna put my hand right here. You like that?"

"Yes."

I kept my eyes open while she kissed my neck. My body shook when she got to my lips. We stayed locked till she let me go. But I didn't want to be let go so I grabbed her by the waist and pulled her back. Now her body shook. We stayed that way till I felt Ever watching through a slit in the door.

Ever. Watching and maneuvering to what end? The universe seemed to bend to her will with the simple flip of her hair. The universe and everything in it, submitting to this kid who wasn't old enough to drink the wine she had before bed every night.

"Aww, was that your first kiss, Jericho?"

Candace was already out of the tub.

"We're going to Ashley's b-day party. I'd invite you, but Mom would flip. Plus, I'm sure you had enough action for one night, wouldn't you say?"

Candace was up the stairs to Ever's room. That was my life, and that wasn't my first kiss. Ever knew that, but that didn't matter. I'd already moved on. I knew what that was and I knew it probably wouldn't happen again. Ever just had this way of shoving things down my throat and forcing me to swallow or choke.

WHEN CANDACE AND EVER got back home, I heard them giggling in the kitchen, then Ever going down the steps to the cellar to grab a new bottle. I heard the cork pop. I'm not sure what I was expecting.

I was still awake when they walked past my door. I saw the shadows of their feet underneath. I knew one of the shadows stopped moving and I was praying she would open the door.

*Do it. I'm still awake.*

Another door closed. The shadow was gone, but my eyes stayed open. It's amazing how much you can see when it's dark. My curtains were pulled, the lamp turned off hours before yet I could still see colors in front of me. I'm the opposite of Ever in so many ways. I dream every single night.

## 3.

I HAD FRIENDS GROWING up. People I spoke to and hung out with other than my sister. There was Prince and Manjit. They're twin brothers who I've known since elementary school. They were school friends, though, and once the bell rang I'd never see them. They'd say their parents were really strict and didn't like them hanging out with anyone outside of their family. They were Sikhs so everyone thought it was some kind of religious thing, but they lived on my street so I knew they were telling the truth.

Keith was another friend who didn't live on my street, but was a five-minute bike ride away. I'd ride over to his place where he'd be waiting on his bike and we'd pedal through the estates and on to the main roads for hours. He had a sister too, but she was younger. Still, we'd go back and forth about what it was like dealing with a sibling whose only intention was to make our lives hell.

Our sister stories were a bit different, though. His stories would make me laugh so hard I'd have to get off my bike just so I didn't fall on my back. His sister Jenny was the type to pour toilet water in his teacup, or lock all the doors and not let him in until he guessed a made-up password. And she does this in February.

I thought those stories were cute, but Jenny is no Ever. Playing pranks was how I wished my sister expressed whatever fondness she had for her brother. Life would be so much easier if Ever splashed me with cold water while I was in the shower or loosened the cap on the salt shaker at dinner.

Then there was James. James was probably the best of all my friends, but the worst influence. He made me cut class in elementary school just so everyone would freak out. We were across the street hiding behind some bushes when we saw teachers outside flooding out of the front doors yelling our names. James thought it was hilarious. My dad flipped out. That was just the beginning.

When I told James about me smoking weed for the first time, he got excited.

"About time," he said. He started calling me more regularly and giving me rendezvous points. He actually used those words. The thought of us getting away with smoking without any of our parents knowing gave James almost as much of a high as smoking the joint.

"It was Candace, wasn't it?"

We were pedaling slowly through the backstreets in our neighborhood. James had the joint in his mouth and was trying to light it. I told him we should wait till we got a few streets over so none of our parents' friends would catch us.

"What do you mean?"

"The reason you took your first pulls. You didn't wanna say no in front of Candace."

"You don't know what you're talking about."

"If you say so."

I wanted to tell him it was more to impress my sister than Candace, but that was weird so I left it alone.

"You try any other drugs?"

"Like what?"

"Like any other drug. You know; coke, percs, zans, molly. Anything like that."

"No, never tried any of those."

"Not one?"

"Naw."

James looked at me the way a straight boy looks at a girl right before he loses his virginity. I wasn't as anxious to get into all that.

All you had to do was go to one pharm party to understand how bored we really were. Picking all different types of pills one by one out of a bowl without really giving a shit which pill we took. Tripping off acid and shrooms. How far could we really go?

I've been to these parties and stuck to the vodka. Just enough to get me buzzed before I'd sneak out and head home before the night turned into a Tim Burton movie. It wasn't the make out sessions or the bedroom noises that got you. That was regular teenager stuff. The craziest part for me was watching everyone transform. At pharm parties especially, you were doing these drugs all night. One after the other, one after the other, pill after pill till you were zombied out.

That was what scared me, and probably why it took till the summer before tenth grade before I tried anything other than weed. That might sound young, but when you're living the type of life where you can get anything you want, anything you want gets old really quickly. It meant that by twelve you were smoking weed, thirteen you've popped your first pill, fourteen you were dropping acid and swallowing shrooms, and by fifteen you've already been doing lines for a full year.

So I was what you called a late bloomer. I'd say a lot of that was because we didn't grow up with a nanny. Our parents figured out a way to be present all the time so we didn't have carte blanche type of freedom. And not saying our parents were strict at all, but they were there. And sometimes just being there was all the deterrence you needed. Privilege and youth are a dangerous mix and I held out as long as possible.

But you can only hold out for so long before blending into your environment. The Rome effect. We lived in our own world. We lived in the real world too, but the life we lived was nothing like the life everyone else lived and we knew it. We stuck together. So while some part of me was proud of myself for resisting for that long, the other side of me always knew it was inevitable. There were only so many times you could say, "I'm good," before you started wondering why the hell you're trying to be good.

"I'll try it." That's how it starts. Three simple words that take your world and spin it like a Ferris wheel round and round and round till you're so fucking dizzy you have no idea where you are or what's been happening. And when the world finally stops spinning, you're back at the front of the line to jump on that Ferris wheel again.

"We have a first timer!" To think that the only time anyone ever cheered for me was the first time I did hard drugs. It was still summer when James and I hit up Keith's birthday party and half the school was at his house. Who knew where his parents were, and I knew he had a nanny, but she wasn't there either. It also looked like some of the tables I remember being in his living room were gone too. And even with so many people there, it wasn't crowded. You could walk without bumping into anyone or find spots to have full conversations without anyone hearing what you were talking about.

James and I were making our rounds through Keith's home, James high fiving and waving to everyone like the cool kid that he was. James had those Travis Scott-type braids that he always talked about chopping off. They would dangle in front of his face and cover his eyes so you could never really tell how he felt about something. Dreamy was the word you'd hear whispered in our school hallways. That was how I knew he'd never even trim the edges, much less cut them all off.

We'd already drank a molly-laced water bottle full of fruit punch on our walk over to Keith's. It only took a few minutes after getting there before I was dodging shadows and counting the number of heads in the room. A few minutes after that, the shadows started looking more and more like characters from the book we were reading in English class. No, maybe the book from my mom's library, or maybe the characters were actually from that episode of Dragon Ball Z I watched that morning.

For the few of you who have never tried MDMA or molly or whatever you want to call it, it's a fucking trip. I wish someone had told me that it was probably a good idea that your first time taking a psychedelic should be done in a much more controlled environment. The madness of having dozens of screaming teenagers around with music blasting and endless supplies of alcohol made me feel like I could walk through walls. It was like I was Rogue from X-Men sucking up everyone's else's energy.

Rolling.

I could taste the scent of shampoo of every girl that walked past me. The wall I leaned up against felt like a soft pillow. The bass from the music flowed through this pillow and into my chest, through my heart and back out again. I saw the vibrations of every person that said, "what's up." Now every shadow was a dancing ninja.

When I came to, I was leaning against the staircase. James was in full conversation about pouring shots for everyone but no one wanted to do it.

"I'll do it."

"You'll do what?"

"Pour the shots."

"Pour what shots? You want someone to get you a shot?"

"We're all doing shots!" I said. More cheers. James is trying his best not to blurt out laughing. Everyone else seems happy.

"All right first-timer, let's do some shots."

"Who's getting it?" James' willpower caved. He curled over laughing, holding his belly the whole time.

I was rolling again.

When I came to, I was holding a shot glass. Everyone was holding a shot glass. I lifted my glass then took the shot quickly. I was already this far in, might as well take it all the way. Another round was being poured.

"How many is that?" I asked James.

"Round five."

"What do you mean round five? Did I miss the first four rounds?"

James just looked at me.

Rolling again. Rolling, rolling, rolling.

Candace was there. She was wearing a loose white dress with a pink flower pinned to the heart side of her chest. She held my hand. Her face was veiled and she was holding my hand. I saw a tear coming down her face.

"Candace. Candace, what's wrong? What's happening? Hey. Talk to me. Candace!"

I WAS ROLLING. ROLLING, rolling, rolling.

My mother was on both knees. Her hands were clasped together and she was looking to the sky.

"Mother?" I was calm now.

"Mother." Something was going on. Something was happening.

"Mom, what the fuck? Answer me! Answer me!"

Rolling. Slowly. Rolling.

# PART II

## JERICHO

MOM SHOULD BE HOME by now. She's at one of those hot yoga classes that she's been going to a lot lately, but she said she's coming right back. It's been about six months since Dad died and Mom has this thing where she tells us exactly where she's going and when she's coming back. At first it felt kind of strange, but now if she's not home within five minutes of when she says she'd be, I'm ready to call her cell.

Ever and I are sitting on the porch when we finally see Mom's SUV pull up. She's not really pulling up, actually. Her car's moving so slow it looks like someone's pushing it. Mom's usually pretty heavy on the gas, but maybe she's on the phone or something. The engine's still running and Mom's not getting out. Ever's already walking down the driveway when Mom finally opens the door. She's holding the left side of her face with her right hand and walking towards us.

"I can't see." Mom's saying this like she's asking a question. "Ever? Jericho? I can't see anything from this eye." The car door's still open. Ever runs towards Mom just as she falls to the ground.

"Mom!" Now we're both beside Mom trying to get her to her feet.

"My leg," she says. "I can't feel my leg."

I look at Ever and she already has her phone out. Mom isn't getting up. She's sitting up on her bum with both legs stretched out, but if we weren't holding her up she'd probably be on her back. We keep her that way till the ambulance comes. Our neighbor John was driving by and saw us huddled around Mom and now he's helping us lift her up till the paramedics take over and strap her onto the gurney.

Ever and I jump in his car and follow the ambulance to the hospital. It's a replay of a memory we both haven't forgotten yet. One we thought we'd never have to deal with again. Not this soon, anyway. Not like this.

Ever's shaking. We're both in the backseat afraid of our own thoughts, but Ever can't seem to control her body. I think I should say something. She would say something consoling to me if she saw me struggling like I think she is right now.

"Don't touch me." That's Ever's reaction to me trying to put my hand on her shoulder. She looks straight at me when she says it. "Don't look at me, don't touch me, don't say anything to me."

The ride to the hospital is short. We had already heard one of the paramedics whisper, "possible stroke," but I'm not sure that meant much to us. It didn't to me. Even though I kind of knew what a stroke was, I didn't know what it looked like. So weeks later when Mom finally comes home in a wheelchair, the entire left side of her face frozen still, her hair shaved off and not able to speak coherently or walk straight, I don't even know what to think.

The sounds are different in our home now. I hear Mom grunt-ing through another physiotherapy session. I hear Grandma and Grandpa talking quietly to each other and stop when I walk in. They've come from British Columbia to help take care of Mom. I don't hear anything from Ever. She moves around our home with-out saying anything to anyone. She comes home right after school now and heads to her room. Mom's parents would worry, but they don't have the energy. Their daughter is their main concern now. As much affection as they've shown us growing up, I know Mom is the only thing on their minds.

But I'm watching Ever. She's around our mother, but rarely close enough to hold her hand or play with her hair when it starts growing back in. She's just watching Mom from the other couch like she's on the set of a reality show. She stares and I'm not even sure she's blinking. Sometimes I'll see tears build up in her eyes before she runs up to her room again, still without a word.

Candace is over today. She's the only one who's gotten more than two words out of Ever since we held Mom in the driveway. So when I hear them speaking in Ever's room, I stand just outside the door.

"She'll never be the same," Ever says. "Maybe we'll drink wine under our pergola again. Maybe she'll be able to do yoga again, but she'll never be the same. It's not fair."

Ever's speaking through soft sniffles. Candace isn't doing much talking herself. She's just letting Ever go off.

"Like why the fuck would this happen to Mom? All she's done is be the perfect parent our whole lives. Dad just died and now she has to deal with this. It's not fair, Candace."

Nothing changes over the next few months. We watch our mother struggle through daily rehab. We sit in the other room as she learns to take steps again. We try our best to mask our faces when Mom is working with the speech person. But nothing could've prepared me to see my mom so helpless. Not even losing a father. In some ways dealing with Mom's illness and recovery has become even more difficult than managing Dad's death. He's gone, and even though it's impossible to process, the truth is we don't see him anymore. At least not physically.

We still see Mom every day. We watch the nurse pushing her around our home in a wheelchair even though Mom is capable now of pushing herself. We try not to ask her to repeat herself too much when she opens half of her mouth to speak. And that's on the rare occasion she actually speaks. She still prefers writing short notes on a small whiteboard she keeps on her lap with an erasable red marker twiddling between the fingers of her strong hand.

*Tired.*

*Hungry.*

*Check on Ever for me.*

*I want to be alone.*

She brushes these statements off with the base of her hand before writing another in the same spot. We do as we are told without question. There's no room for discussion. Not past the sympathy we feel for watching our mother being rolled around silently in a home that has had ramps installed and a makeshift room created on the main floor so Mom won't have to climb the stairs. Sometimes I think that adjusting isn't such a foreign concept for my mother. Dad told us the same story endless times about meeting my mother alone at Horseshoe Tavern in Toronto on St. Patty's Day and Mom eventually making the ultimate adjustment. The last time he told this story was a week before he died. We were all in the backyard that evening, drinking teas and lattes and watching Dad gazing at Mom with that annoying look of pride on his face.

"I thought to myself, who the heck goes to Horseshoe by themselves on St. Patty's?" Dad said. "She was just sitting on a stool at the bar, two shots in front of her and a cup of beer in her hand. How could I not speak to this woman?"

He did speak to her, and it turned out my mother wasn't alone.

"So here I go. After finally catching her eye, I walk right up to her and ask what she's drinking. Before she even answers, here comes this monster of a man right behind her."

I still don't know what my dad was thinking. Why would she be alone? This story only made sense because it was my dad telling it. He wasn't a guy that recognized any social cues, or maybe recognized them but didn't pay attention. So for him, seeing a beautiful woman sitting on her own for thirty seconds was all the cue he needed to approach.

"So now I'm standing there, and he's standing there, your mom is in the middle of us trying her best to not blurt out laughing. This is like straight out of the movies, I'm not kidding. So in this moment of awkwardness, I try to be polite and shake this guy's hand. He looks at me and says, 'I'd rather kiss that hand than kiss her lips. She's all yours, buddy.'"

I can hear Dad laughing out loud at this part. Everyone else would be rolling our eyes, but Dad didn't care. He fought for her. Dad always wanted us to know that. And it wasn't a fight against her parents who thought no one was good enough for their daughter and worried about "leeches" only marrying into the family for a payout. Grandma loved Dad the first time Mom finally introduced them over a year and a half into their relationship. That may seem like a long time, but relationships weren't something my mom was really fond of. Not the kind of relationships they expected back then. Meet girl. Court girl. Marry girl. Mom wasn't into any of that and that's really what my dad was up against.

"'My heart can't belong to any one person,'" Dad said. "That's what she told me the first time I took her out after we met. We walked through Casa Loma smoking a joint and talking about our crazy Prime Minister. Then she drops this polyamorous bomb on me. I'm telling you, it was the most memorable first date I've ever had."

For years my mother kept seeing other men. When she introduced my dad to her parents, he was her main, but still not her only. When my dad proposed the first time, she turned him down.

"I had to take a step back after that. Even though she told me a million times that she's never getting married, or that slitting her wrists with a dull blade was more appealing than settling down and having kids, I still went for it and it still hurt like hell when she said no."

And Mom didn't budge. They went months without speaking to each other after that. Then one day my dad just showed up on her doorstep and said, "Ring or no ring, you're the only one I could ever love."

"We got married a year later." Dad always winked when he said that. It made him feel good to know that he got what he wanted. No, it made him feel good that he got my mom to stretch far enough to let him take her hand. He always loved her, but they both were in love with only each other. That was my mom's first adjustment.

We were her next adjustment. Dad wanted a big family and Mom didn't even want a puppy.

"No offense, guys, but Mom really didn't want either of you." The smirk never left Dad's face when he said this. "If you two ever really knew what it took for you to be here right now ..." That was actually something I'd never heard him say before. We've heard versions of our birth stories from both Mom and Dad. The letter Mom wrote for Ever, then stories of my birth being painless. We've heard so many variations that we never knew which to believe. But when Dad said that, it stuck with me. It's like there was another story waiting to be told.

Either way, that was my mom's second adjustment. Now here she is again being forced to adjust to something that isn't rooted in any emotion. This disease didn't love my mom, but is just as persistent, just as determined to infiltrate her life as my father was to get her to say I do. And she did. She said, "I do" and took that first step towards a life she had sworn would never be hers. Then she took it a step further and had a child. Then another. Two reminders of why her adjustments were worth it.

But this. This needing to be waited on and wheeled around by someone else. This depending on others to feed her and help her pull down her panties in the bathroom was a shift my mother wasn't accepting. From the very beginning, Mom shut down Dad's suggestion of hiring maids or nannies. She refused to be chauffeured around as long as both her hands and feet worked right. Absolutely no joint account with my dad. These are our children, this is my money, this is our home. She kept that separation for her sanity and now that same sanity is being threatened by a sickness she's struggling to conquer.

It hurts. We all see that. And I'm not talking about the physical pain because my mom could deal with that. She's broken collarbones and torn ligaments in her ankles without missing a step. She's dislocated her finger in a tennis match, snapped it right back in place, and kept playing. But psychologically, Mom is feeling the hurt of losing what makes her who she is. Grandma and Grandpa know that. It's why they spend more time trying to lift her spirit rather than catering to her requests. They never push Mom in her wheelchair. "You can get that yourself," is what they say every time Mom asks for something she can reach herself. And even when they first came here after Mom got out of the hospital, they didn't speak to her any differently than they would when they came by for a regular visit.

But Mom's expression isn't changing. We take her for walks out past our backyard near the woods, something she did religiously before the stroke, no change. Grandma plays Nirvana and Madonna and even sits through an entire Tupac song without any commentary. No change. Even when we pull out the big guns and watch Dave Chappelle, someone who makes my mother slap the couch with laughter, nothing. No change.

Nothing changes when Grandma and Grandpa leave. The doctors say my mom shouldn't need the wheelchair as much anymore. They say with the rehab she did at the hospital paired with the daily physiotherapy she's been doing since she's been home, there should be significant improvement in her strength. But here we are months later and Mom's still being rolled around every day. Her favorite note to write on the whiteboard is, "I want to be alone." We all happen to be in the kitchen today with Chef cooking up some French toast. As soon as we're finished eating, Mom uncaps her marker to start writing on the board. Ever sees what's happening, calmly walks up to Mom and snatches the whiteboard away. She opens our front door and tosses it in the driveway.

"If you wanna be alone, go outside and get it," Ever says. "If it's still out there when I'm out of the bathroom, I'm going to take my car and drive over it until it's in a million little pieces."

We all watch with our mouths open as Ever walks upstairs to her room, then comes back down minutes later with the car keys dangling in her hand. I can't help walking to the front window to see her start her car and drive over the whiteboard, then reverse and drive over it again. She does that two or three times before turning off the ignition, then gets out of the car and skips up the driveway and through the front door.

"Guess there's no more alone time," Ever says to Mom.

I tell Grandpa that story and he calls Grandma and puts me on speaker phone so I could tell it again.

"Good for her," Grandma says. "It's about time your mother stops feeling sorry for herself and starts being a mother again."

It's the evening now and we're streaming season two of the Chappelle Show.

"Mom?" I say in the middle of a "When Keeping It Real Goes Wrong" scene. "Mom, what's the matter?" There's a tear dripping down the frozen side of her face. "Mom," I say again without getting any reaction. Ever walks into the living room and sits on the opposite end of the sectional.

"Mom," she says. "Are you OK?"

Mom's face starts to twitch just slightly. The top of either side of her lips begins to curl. She puts her right hand to her mouth and lets out a sound that none of us have heard for months. Ever and I glance over at each other. We look back at Mom in time to see her slap the couch and hold onto her tummy to let out her familiar belly laugh. A month after that, Mom ditches the wheelchair for good. A little while after that, she could walk beyond our backyard and both sides of her face move when she speaks.

Ever's been bouncing around since that belly laugh day. She's not walking around like she lost something anymore. Something she hid a long time ago and has no idea where to find it. Now she's telling me she doesn't like the color of my sweater and that I need to put on socks so she doesn't have to bear looking at my toes. Or that I should either cut my hair or let it grow out because I look like a character in a video game.

Before any of this happened, I never thought of anyone dying or being sick. Or at least I didn't think that kind of stuff would happen to my family. You hear about those things on the news. You hear about that stuff from your friends at school. Only in other families are things like divorce and heart attacks and strokes possible, not in ours.

But when Mom had her stroke and almost died, and then struggled through recovery for months, part of me felt stupid for thinking the world would somehow skip the tragedy in our family. It's not like I still don't believe that I can be anything and do anything I want. That I can try things, love it, get over it, try something else and continue this kind of cycle endlessly. But there's a part of my childhood that's gone forever. Like getting pubic hairs for the first time or the first time I recognized that being cool was a thing. I never looked at the world the same after those events and Dad dying and Mom having a stroke had the same kind of impact on me, but on a much deeper level.

"Do they recycle wheelchairs?" It's one of those conversations Ever wishes she didn't have to tolerate from a little brother. We're in the car on the way to Shoppers Drug Mart. Ever's driving and I'm being a little brother.

"What are you even talking about, Jericho?"

"Wheelchairs. Do you think they recycle them?"

"Who cares?"

"Mom doesn't have her wheelchair anymore so I just think they should recycle them."

"I think you should stop talking." And I try.

"Are you happy Mom is alive?" Ever asks. I think the question is strange, but Ever asking me the question is even more alarming.

"Huh? What do you mean?"

"Like you saw what she went through. That was so crazy and for what? She wasn't a bad person, she never tried to hurt anyone, Mom barely even swears. But for some reason, the universe thought it was OK to make her go through that. That's bullshit."

"But she's alive. That's better than not being alive."

"But she's not the same. She'll never be the same. No matter what, she just won't be the same person. You're OK with that?"

"So you rather she be dead?"

"That's not what I'm saying. You know what, forget it. This is not a conversation I should be having with you."

But she is having it with me which means she isn't having it with anyone else. And if this experience had stolen away a piece of my childhood naïveté, it's completely taken away Ever's trust in the universe.

But I blow it off. Ever is my older sister. Love her some days, hate her most, but I'll always look up to her. I even admire her in a lot of ways. The older I get, the more I realize how difficult it is to say exactly how you feel. People pacify their thoughts, their words. They even act a certain way to avoid people saying stuff about them, even if the stuff they would say is true.

Ever never has that problem. She always says whatever's on her mind and does what she wants. But with Mom finally recovering from her stroke, it's hard to tell what Ever is feeling most of the time. It looks like she's happy to have Mom back to normal. Or somewhat back to normal. But then she tells me that Mom isn't normal and will never be the same again. "Who cares" is what I think to myself. I'll take a limping mother who hates that she's put on thirty pounds and still slurs some words over not having a mother at all. Any kid would.

The thing is though, Ever is not just any child. She was already thinking about quality of life before I started seeing it on a bunch of blog posts in high school. So even though she's back to doing Mom's hair and giggling with her on the couch, there's another side to her that asked me that question.

Regardless of what Ever thinks, Mom is getting her life back. The day she got rid of her wheelchair was the first day she started planning a party. We were eating lunch together on the couch in the living room when my mom first told us about the idea.

"We're about to do a lot of celebrating this year, guys. Get ready for it." Not a problem for us. In fact, I had one of my few bright ideas when I asked Mom if we could double down on the party and make it a celebration of Dad's life.

"The funeral was so sad," I said. "Everyone was crying and talking about how much they'll miss him. Dad was always happy. He always had a smile on his face and a funny story to tell. He would be happy if we threw him a big party."

My mother looked at me like I was Ever.

"That's the best idea I've heard all year. Yes! We're throwing a celebration of life party. Great idea, Jericho. Amazing. Come here." Even Ever had to give it up to me after that one. She gave me a head nod and we did that stupid handshake we made up when we were like seven and eight or something.

"Dad would love this," Ever said. "He'd probably be like, 'kick-ass, Jericho. Let's groove it out.'" Laughter.

"No, no, wait. He'd say, 'Dude, you just fucking killed it. Hell yeah.'" More laughing.

"Wait, I got it. Your dad would be like, 'Hey hun, we keeping the kids here for this party or is it actually gonna be fun?'" We were all in tears. Funny how laughing too much makes you cry. It's like emotions are just emotions and we're the ones who categorize them. Something like that.

The party is going much better than we could've planned. Mom decided to make it an all-white dress code to stress the point that this really is a celebration of life. All the neighbors who Mom invites show up in white dresses and pantsuits, big white hats with touches of color on the appendages. The guys are wearing white suits or white shirts with white jean pants and white shoes with colored laces. The only thing missing is Ryan Seacrest on the red carpet asking everyone who they're wearing.

All guests are ushered into our backyard by the usual staff my mom hires for our events. A bar is set up in the corner closest to the house and servers are carrying around seafood and vegetarian dishes for most of the evening. When guests first arrive, they're handed a glass of champagne with a small card. The card fits neatly inside most people's clutches or pockets and each of them include a message handwritten by my mother. For family and close friends, Mom writes short, personal messages. One-liners that speak to something they shared together.

*Desiree, the day we met is the day fun was introduced to my life.*

*Pete, tears at 2:00 a.m. is better than ice cream.*

*Rose, you know you're that bitch.*

For everyone else, she pulls sayings from *A Year with Rilke*. Overall, she writes close to 100 messages.

Halfway through the evening, Mom steps to the front of our yard and taps her glass. She looks strong standing at the head of the crowd, dressed in Dad's favorite yellow dress she only tried on once in the bedroom when my father fell in love with it.

"What a wonderful evening," Mom starts. "I asked you all to come here so we could celebrate life and that's exactly what we're doing." Ever nudges through the crowd to stand beside me.

"All my family, all my friends, everyone I care about, in some way you've all contributed to making my husband and I feel loved, feel appreciated, and feel like we're part of something special. I know he's looking down on us right now and feeling all the joy inside his home. And he's smiling because this is the way he would want to be celebrated."

"This has been a rough stretch for our family. When my husband passed, I wondered how I'd be able to carry on. He was such a caring spirit with a heart so big, it stored enough love for everyone in this room. His passion for life, the love he had for his children ... No one is perfect, but he came pretty damn close, I'll tell you."

Ever is mouthing the words with my mother. They were up in Mom's room the night before, rehearsing. I fell asleep listening to them rearrange and remove lines, trying to get it perfect. The end of Mom's speech was the only part I remembered from last night.

"Before I let you all get back to drinking, I'd like to say one more thing. My husband may be gone, but he's left me with so much. A home, enough money to last two lifetimes, and God knows I already had enough money, right Dad? But he also left me with two incredible kids who are both so gifted, so independent, and who share their father's heart. It truly is a blessing to watch them grow and form into their own people. They kept me going when I couldn't find the strength to move on. None of this would've been possible without my husband. Our children are a result of his persistence, commitment, and dedication to building this family. Cheers."

## CANDACE

"SHE'S STILL NOT HERSELF." Ever's flopped on her bed with headphones around her neck. We just got back from school and she talked like this the entire walk.

"I don't get what you expect from her," I say. "She had a stroke, Ever. And she's doing pretty damn good now. Maybe you should chill."

"Why? Why should I chill? Is being alive the bar for having a good life?"

"You don't think your mom has a good life?"

Ever doesn't say anything. I sit on the bed beside her with my knapsack still on.

"Maybe it's you," I say.

Ever flips over from her stomach to her back and tosses her headphones to the side.

"What do you mean maybe it's me? You think I'm the one who had a stroke?"

I slap Ever playfully on her belly and she fakes like it hurt. "I mean maybe you have a problem."

She sits up and looks at me like I just told her that the sky is orange.

"Why would I have a problem? I'm not sick." I don't get this girl sometimes. She's by far the smartest person I know, but the things that are right in front of her face are the furthest from her mind.

I slept on Ever's bed every night for a month when her dad died. She cried herself to sleep the first two weeks. When her mom had a stroke, I was at the hospital that same day. Ever was sitting beside Jericho shaking like her body just couldn't get warm. Jericho was staring at her. I could tell he was just as scared for Ever as he was for his mom. The neighbors that followed the ambulance with Ever and Jericho in the back were pacing close by. They were a younger couple which was weird for where we lived because most adults in our area already had some grays. These two looked like they still made out in public.

I wrapped my arms around Ever right away while my mom spoke to the neighbors. Ever was still sitting and didn't even look at me. I remember thinking that she wasn't this broken when her dad was in the hospital, but I think pain was still new to her then. Both her grandparents were still alive (Ever never knew her dad's parents, neither did he from what I heard), she never got broken up with by a boy she liked, I don't even think Ever's been stung by a bee. So when it finally sunk in that her dad was gone, then a few months later her mom suffered a stroke, she had more than enough reason to be blank-faced and trembling when I saw her in the hospital that day.

And that's what I'm trying to tell her now; maybe she's the one with the problem. I was only five when my fake mom left and

I still get mad thinking about her. If the stuff that happened to Ever happened to me, I don't know what I'd do.

"I know you're not sick. Not like that, anyway. I'm just saying that maybe your mom getting sick so soon after you losing your dad is hard for you to deal with."

"Of course it's hard. It's fucking impossible. But what am I supposed to do about it?"

"Talk to someone," I say. And as I say it, I already know Ever's reaction. We know about those girls. Those girls who talk to people. Professional people. We don't talk about it unless they do and when they do we tell them how brave they are, how much we support them and that we're sorry they have to go through that.

In our mind, though, we convince ourselves that we'll never be them. That there's nothing that would ever push us to open up our lives and our feelings to some stranger. Someone outside of the friendship that Ever and I have built. "We have each other," Ever says, and holds her left hand out, palm down. I put my right hand over it and we'd say "sisters," in unison.

"You know that's never gonna work," Ever says. "Talking to someone isn't gonna fix anything."

"Yeah, you're probably right, but ... I don't know. Maybe you should think about it."

As I'm directing these words to Ever I wonder how much of it is really meant for me. I know I say I don't care about my fake mother, and I don't, but I still think about her. I always have. Even though I'm in my last year of high school and haven't seen her since I stopped peeing my bed, something's still there.

Mom tries her best to create a shield around me. I can't blame her. I would be protective too, if I had walked into an apartment and held a five-year-old child who'd been alone for two days. What would it take to rip the memory of my fake mother out of my head? The weird thing is the older I get, the angrier I get. When I was eight or nine I didn't even care. The only person I'd ever speak to about her was Ever, and that stopped once there wasn't any more to tell.

"You can be mad, Candace." That was Mom when I was still in grade six. She picked me up from school and had that concerned parent look on her face. Apparently, I said something to my teacher about having a fake mom. The teacher looked at me like my mom was looking at me parked in the schoolyard and thought it wise to call her. "Being mad is normal. Especially with what you've been through."

"I'm not mad, Mommy. I don't care about my fake mother. I don't even think about her."

That wasn't enough to stop the prodding. Mom asked me about how I was getting along with my friends at school, if I ever felt left out, if she ever made me feel like I didn't belong. When we got to our driveway, she shut off the car, took off her seatbelt, and turned her whole body towards me.

"I don't ever want you to feel like you're not special, Candace. If there's ever something bothering you or if you don't feel happy about something in your life, just let me or your dad know."

It's funny because when I hear Mom tell her friends this story today, she always tells it as a joke. Probably because the last thing I said to her when she went all helicopter mom on me was, "Mom, I go horseback riding. My life is fine."

And it was. How many little girls have fucked up parents or no parents at all and have no choice but to endure it? They have to swallow the poverty and the depression, the violence and the neglect. It's exhausting. Then here I come and for whatever reason, I was taken out of that miserable life and given a way better one.

I always knew how lucky I was. Because that's all it was; pure luck. Mom hated hearing that.

"You weren't supposed to be possible, Candace."

It was the same day as the school thing. Mom and I were eating popcorn in the living room after watching one of those Jason movies. She hated getting scared and closed her eyes through most of it, but was always the one suggesting we put it on.

"Our family, this family, none of this was supposed to happen. I didn't find you in that room, you were given to me."

She doesn't ever want to let that go. That moment meant so much to her. So much so that she made a conscious decision not to have any more children. Even though there's nothing wrong with her physically, Mom made a choice that I would be her only child. When I got into my teenage years and started asking her why she never had any more kids, she always said, "because God gave you to me." She's been protecting me ever since. And not just my body, Mom protected my psyche just as aggressively.

*Protect your mind.*

She posted this saying on the inside of my bedroom door when I first moved in. I had no idea what it meant for the first few years, but I kept it. It's still here now in alternating yellow and green block letters.

"People can take everything away from you except your mind. Protect it, Candace. At all costs."

Mom is full of these doomsday quotes. When I accuse her of

being nihilistic, she says she can't be because hope is at the center of her soul.

I get it though. I know why she taped that quote up on my door. She wanted me to be ready. When the guilt and hatred started pulling me to a place I knew I didn't want to be, I repeated my mother's words.

But actually getting help? Speaking to a therapist? That's not something I'm up for. Or at least I don't think I'm up for it. Because what do I really have to complain about? Even in sixth grade I knew my life was privileged. Yet here I am telling Ever to get help dealing with her dad dying and with everything going on with her mom.

"We're sisters, right Candace?" How long was I zoned out for? I almost forget we're still in Ever's room.

"Of course."

"No matter what?"

"Why you talking like this?"

"I'm just saying. If you found out I did something really messed up, we'd still be sisters, right?"

"You can kill someone and we'd still be sisters. But I'm not burying any bodies."

"That's good to know." I'm waiting for Ever to say more, but she stops. There's something, though. I don't know what it is, but it's something.

The next morning, I wake up to four missed calls from Ever. We never call each other so I know something's up. But it's Saturday morning and whatever it is can wait. At least that's what I think till Ever barges through my bedroom door.

"I got it," she says. I cover my face with my blanket, but Ever pulls it off. "Did you hear what I said? I said I got it."

Ever's standing at the foot of my bed waiting for me to say something. She hustles to the drapes and pulls them open and that gets me to sit up.

"OK, let me hear it." Even though I'm still tired and annoyed and my eyes are barely open, I can't help but share some of Ever's excitement. I have no idea what she's about to say, but there's not too much that gets her energy up like this so it must be something big.

"Boys and Girls Screaming," she says.

"What are you talking about?"

"Boys and Girls Screaming. That's what we're gonna call our group."

"What group?"

"The group we're gonna start. We're actually gonna call it BAGS for short, but that's what it stands for. It's gonna be our own support group. Like, who needs therapists. We can help each other."

I don't know what my face looks like right now but Ever's is beaming. She still has her head-tie on, the yellow and green one of course, and is wearing the sweatsuit I bought for her birthday last year.

"OK. So we're starting a support group?"

"Something like that," Ever says. "I'm not sure if that's the right terminology or whatever, but yeah. It's gonna be us. Kids helping kids. Trust me, this is gonna work."

If any other teenager said this, I would grab my blanket and go back to bed. But this is not any other teenager. Ever's someone who actually follows through on the stuff that she talks about. Like that time she said she's going to get fluent in French before her parents took her to France. This had to be grade seven. I didn't even remember she said that till a month before the trip when I heard her speaking to one of our school friends on the phone in full Français. She did that in less than a year. I tried for a week after that before deleting all those language apps on my phone.

That was five years ago. Over that time, she's also managed to gather a small army of followers on social media. I thought she had fans in middle school, but now her Instagram's almost into the six digits.

@EverAfter. Don't ask me how she got that handle. It's actually strange being her friend sometimes. We'd go out somewhere and someone from a different high school recognizes her, or she'd get invited to listening parties in New York even though she can't go. Sometimes she gets free tickets to these random bands we've never heard of, but when we go to their show, hundreds of people are there singing along to every single song.

So yeah, if she says she wants to start this group, we're doing this group.

"Who are we supporting in this group?" I ask. "Can anyone join?"

"Of course not. This group is for kids who've gone through some kind of trauma. Like me and you, know what I mean. Maybe they lost a parent or were abandoned by a parent. Or maybe they came from another country or something where they saw people get shot and killed and it's still messing with them."

"OK, and only kids?"

"Only high school kids," Ever says. "And we're gonna choose the ones we ask to participate. At least at first. We have to see how it goes before we open it up to more people."

Of course she has everything figured out. She tells me she stayed up all night working out the details.

"We're gonna use your basement because it has the right vibe. You should probably let your mom know. I've already picked out four kids in our school who fit the criteria. Plus, you can ask that girl you tell me about, the one you met at that photoshop class you take. She sounds like she could use some help."

Ever's scrolling through notes on her phone while she's pacing around my room. I'm up now too, feeling more energized than I should at eight in the morning.

"We should probably have some rules, right?" I say. "So everyone knows what to expect and no one feels like their business is gonna be all over school."

"I thought about that and came up with a few. Whatever we say in the group stays in the group. That's the first rule. No drinking or anything else during the session. We wait till after till we do any of that. And the only other rule I came up with is that no one should feel pressure to say anything. If they wanna sit there and be a spectator until they're ready to open up, then so be it."

"Those are good ones. How often are we gonna meet?"

"I'm thinking, like, once a week. Maybe after school so we're not asking anyone to give up time on their weekends."

Ever says we'll meet for an hour, but if we need more time then we'll take it.

"However long it takes for someone to get through their shit. We're not treating these people like patients on the clock. If it takes three hours for someone to say what they have to say, then that's what it is."

We also decide to start a chat group on IG. That way we can organize our meetups and give our group a chance to continue the conversation.

An hour or so passes before Nanny knocks on the door and hands us a tray with waffles, syrup, some orange juice and chopped up fruit.

"Sounds like you all need some food for the brain," she says. How is it possible that Nanny looks the exact same as the first time I set foot in this house? I don't even see any gray in her dreads. But now that I think about it, I don't even know how old Nanny is.

While we took a quick break to munch out on some breakfast, I see Ever giving me strange looks.

"So," she says. "What's up with you and my little brother?"

She just had to put it like that. "Little" brother. It's only one year, but it makes a difference when the boy's younger, especially as a teenager. And there really is nothing going on with me and Jericho. Not for real, anyway. Ever knows that, but she knows me too. And everyone knows nothing gets past Ever.

To be honest, though, you don't have to be a detective to see what happens when Jericho and I are in the same room. I catch him sometimes. Stealing looks. He thinks I don't notice because I never react, but I see him. Plus, he's starting to hang around us a bit more. He's not scared to take a couple puffs off the joint when Ever and I go on our strolls. It's cute. Even cuter after some purple kush.

I'm sure he feels all grown up now. That's probably why he thinks he has a chance. Little Jericho. He sees the kind of boys I date. Guys who try their hardest not to look like they're trying. Boys who don't play sports and keep whatever fuzz grows on their faces and spend their weekends playing trap music in parking lots out of their cars. But that doesn't mean I want him to stop blushing every time I say hi, or stop pretending that he likes smoking weed even though Ever and I gave him his first joint and he tripped the fuck out. He thinks I forgot about that. It's all about him being cool when he's around us, though, so I never bring it up. I just watch the sheepish way he puts the joint at the tip of his lips and barely inhales. He's trying.

"Don't try to brush me off," Ever says. "You don't usually like the shy, nerdy type. Is he blackmailing you?"

I toss a slice of cantaloupe at Ever's head. She dodges it and pretends to throw one back.

"He's not nerdy. Maybe a little shy, but I think it's kinda cute." I didn't mean to say that second part. I immediately glance over at Ever for a reaction. She's smiling, but that's her thinking face. Behind that front, she's trying to figure out if she's really OK with this. What if Jericho and I actually become a thing? How will she function?

"It's OK, sis. I think my brother's an idiot, but if you like him that's cool. Now that I think about it, if you guys get married, we won't be lying when we say we're sisters."

"Slow down. No one's getting married." But it did cross my mind to tell Ever that Jericho and I made out a few times, among other things. I know his favorite time was in the jacuzzi, but my favorite was in his basement. No one ever goes down there unless they're looking for something to bring back upstairs, but it's all the way done up with a full kitchen and a bar, although most of it is just open space that Cy says is good for meditating and doing yoga. The time that kiss happened with Jericho, Cy asked me to grab a bottle of red and when I turned around, this boy was standing right in front of me. He didn't even say anything. He just grabbed my waist and crashed our lips together.

I tried everything not to drop the bottle of wine, but my body felt so damn weak. He got me that day. I don't know if it was so much the kiss or the balls it took to know I'd kiss him back. He took a chance and nailed it. I had to give him some credit.

It was on after that. I still played it cool, but made sure he knew I wanted more than these random make out sessions. At least I thought I did. Boys are clueless sometimes so he didn't exactly pick up on all the signs. Like I thought inviting him over to my house to watch a movie without Ever there would be clear enough. By the first hour of the movie, I was ready to rip off his shirt, but he was at the other end of the couch sitting up like we both hadn't watched *Bad Boys* a million times already. It took me laying on his lap to get any kind of touch that night, but that was where it ended. I almost gave up, but then he got another sudden bout of confidence the next day and asked me to the cottage for the entire weekend. Like sleeping over.

"The cottage?" I asked. "Sounds like a good time. Who else is coming?"

"You and me, Candace. No one else is coming." I had to keep messing with him.

"Oh. So we'll be alone?"

"Yes, we'll be alone."

"OK, I'll do it on one condition. No couches."

That was one wild weekend. We planned to go bike riding and hiking through the trail he knows I really like, but our first day there, we didn't even make it out. After slipping molly in each other's drink, I went to the bathroom and came out in a gold medal with a red band that I'd won in a photography contest. That killed whatever plans we thought we made.

Actually, it pretty much killed the weekend. Most of it is a haze. We were always so fucked up so staying inside and getting loose with each other made a lot more sense than walking the trails. I didn't mind, though. That's the weekend I first thought that Jericho and I could be a real thing. Not just some kind of high school flame I'd get bored with after a few dates. When we were cuddled together that weekend, I felt something I can't really describe other than to say it felt really good.

"If I knew this is how it would be, I never would've waited this long." It was our last night there and I felt like messing with him.

"Waited?" Jericho said. "You weren't waiting on me."

"No, but we could've got here a lot sooner if you were a bit more ..."

"What? A bit more what?"

"Never mind. We're here now." Poor kid. I should stop. "Did you have a good time?" I asked him this while sparking the joint we outed that morning.

"Why? Is it over already?"

"It doesn't have to be."

"It doesn't? You mean you want to stay here longer?" Girls really do mature faster than boys.

"You're cute when things fly over your head. I'm having second thoughts now. Maybe you're not ready."

"I'm ready for anything, trust me."

On second thought, maybe I'll wait to tell Ever about all that.

We had more important things to worry about. When we got to school the Monday after she barged into my room, we were supposed to divide and conquer. I'm supposed to tell Stacy and Lindsay and Ever's supposed to tell Mark and Desiree. Talking about it all weekend was fun and exciting. Now that I actually had to approach someone face to face, it hit me that we're doing something real.

I wanted to DM everyone, but Ever said we have to do it in person. I'm regretting letting her convince me. Even though we spent Sunday practicing our lines.

*Hey Lindsay, Ever is starting this group called BAGS. It's for kids like us who've been through some kind of family trauma. Like a support group so we can talk and help each other out. Because who knows what we're really going through better than us, right?*

Simple enough, but when I see Lindsay at her locker, I can't remember anything I have to say. She's watching me, watching her with her blue school jacket on. Lindsay's hair is long enough to cover the crest on the chest of her jacket and blonde enough that she's never had to bleach it. There are only a few minutes before last period starts and I know talking to her after school won't work.

"You OK, Candace?" Lindsay asks. "You look like you're holding your breath."

"Yup, I'm good. Actually, I need to ask you something."

When I finally spit it out, Lindsay's staring at me like I was staring at her a few seconds ago. She looks around and moves in a bit closer.

"You mean like group therapy?"

"Not exactly. Well, kinda. We don't really think of it as therapy. It's more like ... I don't know what it's like because we haven't really done it yet. But Ever thinks it can help kids like us and I think it's worth a try. If you have some of the same thoughts that I have, then I know it won't be a waste of time."

Lindsay gives a hesitant nod while I'm talking. She's still looking over my shoulder with every other word. I'm starting to realize just how crazy this plan really is. And trying to convince other kids to come join us to do God knows what might be the craziest part of this plan.

The bell rings, but I can tell Lindsay still has a million more questions.

"Listen," I say. "We're meeting at my house after school on Wednesday. Just come by if you can. I'll add you to our IG group so you can ask all the questions you want."

Lindsay closes her locker and walks away to class. Before I go the other way, she turns around and asks the one question that's safe enough to ask out loud.

"Why is it called BAGS?"

"Boys and Girls Screaming."

# CANDACE

I'VE BEEN FEELING NAUSEOUS all day. I thought about skipping school and staying laid up in bed with my phone off. Ever must've known how I was feeling because she was at my door earlier than usual. By the time we got in her car, I wasn't feeling any better. She wasn't saying much, either, which made me think she was just as sick about this as I was.

Now we're both standing in my basement checking our phones every thirty seconds for someone to message and say they're outside. No one agreed to join the IG group, but Ever said she reached out to everyone individually yesterday and told them they can message me or her personally. Ever's chef cooked up some crab cake appetizers with crackers, slices of pear, and four different kinds of cheese.

We asked everyone to be here by 4:00, but it's almost 4:15 and unless someone messaged in the last twenty seconds, no one's here.

"Did Lindsay say she's gonna make it?" Ever asks.

"Kinda. She didn't say no. I just told her when and where and figured she'd come if she wanted to."

"What about Stacy?"

"She said she'll be here. Want me to message her?"

Ever's staring at her phone doing her best not to look at me. I didn't know how much this meant to her till this moment. We have floor pillows arranged in a circle in the middle of the room. All the food is on the bar ledge which is at the corner furthest from the basement door. Ever's standing beside the bar tapping her fingers on her phone. I'm watching her. She curves her hair behind her ear and checks her phone again.

We really are sisters. And I never thought of this till right now, but if Ever and I were real sisters, I mean blood sisters, we'd be twins. We would've been together from the very spark of life. So many of my best memories are with her. Writing on each other's hands when we first met. The countless conversations in her room that ended in tears. Our weed walks during the summer. Ever's been there every step of the way and always when I needed her most. But now I'm watching her. Still tapping on her phone trying her best not to peek down. I know what she's feeling.

I sit down on one of the floor pillows, cross my legs and reach my hands out.

"Come sit with me," I say. It's the first time she looks at me since we've been down here. She hesitates for a second then puts her phone next to the charcuterie plate and sits down quietly on a pillow right beside me.

"You're pissed, aren't you?" I say.

"Not really." Ever looks back at the bar then back down at the floor in front of her.

"Ever."

"What?"

"You're pissed."

Ever's head lifts just enough for me to see the hazel glint of her eyes from her profile and it finally feels like we're in the same room.

"Sis," I say. "Talk to me." I don't think I've ever said those words to Ever. I've never had to. Ever tells me if her period's a day late or if they put too much milk in her Americano. We've slept curled up, back to belly on the same bed more times than two teenagers probably should. But we've never been here before. Not like this. Not where Ever has something on the line.

"It was a stupid idea," she says. "No one wants to talk about their problems with people they have to see at school the next day." I shift a little closer to Ever and rest my hand on her knee. "I just thought," she says. "I don't know what I thought. Maybe I thought people are struggling and I can actually help. That sounds crazy, right? Like, who am I helping? Of course no one showed up. Why would they?"

Ever's shrinking with every word. I think about telling her she's not crazy. That it's scary for anyone to talk about their shit and that it's not her fault that no one's showing up. But I don't say anything. Ever already knows everything I'm about to say and I can tell she wants to say more.

"I can't stop thinking about Mom." We're still in our school uniforms. Our ties are loosened and our shirts are untucked like always. My jacket's still on, but Ever's tossed hers to the side since she's been talking.

"Every time I look at her, the first thing I think about is that Dad's not here. And I know she's better now, but the next thing I think about is her stroke. Like, that stroke took something from her that she just can't get back. And now all I can see when I look at her is that thing that's missing."

"But she's fine, Ever. Cy's doing everything she did before she had the stroke."

"I know. I try telling myself that, but I can't make myself believe it. I feel like there should've been something I could've done. Something to help Mom when Dad died so she didn't have to carry all that pain and stress on her own. Maybe ..."

Ever let go of my hands.

"I hate it," she says. "And I hate the universe for letting it happen."

## JERICHO

THIS BUTTERFLY WON'T LEAVE me alone. It's gliding over my head, resting on my shoulder, even landing on my chest and staying there for a whole minute. When Candace tries to take a picture on her phone, it flies away. Then it comes back again.

This goes on in the backyard of the cottage for almost an hour, till we spot a family of raccoons creeping by and run inside. Inside, I see the same butterfly close to the window. It's like it knows me, which sounds ridiculous but that's my story. A flap of the wing is all it takes. I remember reading that somewhere, or maybe it was a movie. Something about how everything in the universe is so connected that the single flap of a butterfly's wings could cause a typhoon on the other side of the world.

If only that were true. I don't see how it can be, though. I don't feel connected to shit. I don't even know what the fuck I'm doing with my life. While Ever has a social media army behind her, I'm dodging butterflies and sitting on my laptop looking at universities that would make Mom dance if I ever got accepted.

What have I really been doing all this time? I'm still a year away from graduating, but I don't know what I want to do. My guidance counsellor says I should go into industrial engineering, but I don't even know what that is. I googled it and still don't know what it is.

This isn't life. I wish I could skip to the part where this all makes sense because right now, I don't get it. And it's not like Mom is pressuring me to do anything. "Whatever makes you happy, Jericho. It would be nice if that happiness came with a degree, but it's your life."

Days are passing by. If I'm not high, I want to be. If I'm not out with James, I'm with Candace. Sometimes we're all together and that's always a mess. There's something about the energy of a crowd that could take things either way. James brings Sarah along sometimes too. That's the new girl from Appleby he's been dating since the start of second semester.

Four bored kids at the cottage on the weekend Mom said we can go without her. Shrooms are the group drug of choice this time. It's only April, so it's still cool enough for us to blend the shrooms in tea and trip out on the front porch. Then at night we jump in the hot tub and stare at the stars for what must be hours. Candace is telling us about studying to be in fashion.

"But not the design part," she says. "I'm talking about the business stuff. Buying and selling fashion, marketing the different lines, figuring out how to get expensive clothes in the closets of regular people. That's what I'm talking about."

"Why don't you wanna design?" James doesn't even look down from the stars. "Didn't you used to paint when you were a kid?"

"I still do. I'll always love painting. But after fashion camp last summer, I realized what I want to do with the rest of my life and this is it. I mean, I still wanna wear nice things, I just don't wanna make them."

"I like nice things too," Sarah chimes in.

"I almost drowned once," I say.

"Here we go." Candace hates when I talk about this.

"What? I did. You were there, remember?"

"Of course I remember. We had to take you to the hospital."

"Yeah, that was messed up. I always blamed Ever for that, but, to be real, I was super high. Weed does something to me, especially the first few times I smoked. That's why I stick to psychedelics."

"I'm drowning now," James says and pretends to flail his arms and legs.

"I can't even swim." I think that's Sarah.

Then we get silent. The stars look like they're an arms-length away. Like I can grab them one by one and let them float in the tub beside me. I don't even know how I'm seeing all of this when I'm sure my eyes are closed.

James and Sarah head inside. I don't know how long Candace and I have been dipped in the water, but it's still dark outside so that's a good sign.

"You OK?" She asks. I nod my head slowly, still thinking about collecting stars. "You know what this reminds me of?"

"How can I forget?" I say. "I think about it every day."

"Oh really? One kiss left that much of an impression on you?"

"It wasn't one kiss, it was our first kiss." It's so dark that it's hard for me to make out Candace's full reaction, but I know she's smiling.

"I've been meaning to ask you," I say. "What's up with Ever? She's been acting strange lately."

"What do you mean strange?" I can tell Candace knows what I mean. The way she responded made me think she notices it too and wants to know what I know.

"I mean strange. Like we'll be eating breakfast together and she won't say anything. Or the other day, I asked her to turn down her music so I can do my homework and she actually turned it down."

"And that's a bad thing?"

"It's concerning. Usually, she'd say something slick like, 'You realize that you're not smart, right little bro?' Or, 'Learning just isn't your thing, Jericho.' She didn't say anything like that. Something's up. What do you know?"

Candace turns just enough so the light from inside the cottage brightens a small part of her face, but she still hasn't said anything yet so I know there really is something.

"Does it have to do with that thing you guys were doing at your house last week?" Now it's Candace's turn to nod her head slowly.

"Yes and no, I guess," Candace says. "Last week put her in a mood, but it's a bit deeper than that."

Candace tells me about Ever's idea. This group called Boys and Girls Screaming. She tells me about the hours Ever spent planning and then actually walking up to people and inviting them to come.

"I wanted to throw up in my mouth when we had to do that," Candace says that as plainly as she tells the rest of the story. Then she gets to the part where no one showed up.

"Ever didn't take that too well," she says. "It meant something to her. And you know it's rare for her to care about something that isn't under her roof."

I did know how rare this was for Ever. And I could probably

guess why it meant so much to her, but I don't bother getting into that with Candace. I'm more impressed with the fact that Ever wants to help other people. That she actually thought of an idea, a good idea, and it wouldn't just benefit her.

"I know people who'd wanna come," I say.

"No you don't." I couldn't tell if Candace was being serious or sarcastic. "I mean, we thought we knew people too. But it's not that simple. I just told you we invited like five people and none of them showed up."

"And I'm telling you that I know people who will show up."

"Like who?"

"Like don't worry about it. Just tell me what they have to do."

Candace still isn't convinced. She tells me that if I know people for real, I should get them to join the IG group.

"They can message Ever and she'll add them."

"That's it?"

"That's it."

By the time we get back home on Sunday, I've already messaged four people. Three of them say they'll message Ever and when Candace texts me heart emojis that night I know they all did. I also tell James about it. I don't tell him about messaging Ever, but something tells me he'd be down to give it a try.

"So it's a group where we sit and talk?" James adds the confused emoji after his text. I'm in my room messaging Candace back at the same time.

"Kinda. It's like everyone is gonna share their stories, you know? Just kids. No parents to psychoanalyze the situation."

"I don't know what psychoanalyze means, but it sounds painful."

"LOL, you in or what?"

"Are you doing it too?"

"Naw, Ever's my sister, bro. It'll probably be weird if I'm there."

James agrees and tells me to let him know when and where. I text Candace and she sends me back prayer hands.

The next morning Ever doesn't make it down for breakfast before we leave for school, but when she sees me at the table, she sits at the edge of the chair beside me with her knapsack hanging off one shoulder.

"These people are really gonna show up, right?" She's smiling when she says it, and I smile back with omelette in my mouth.

"They'll be there."

"Good." Ever gets up and heads for the door. "You can come too, Lil Jericho," she says without turning around. "It's in our basement this time, not Candace's." She's out the door before I can say thank you, even though she should technically be the one thanking me, but it's Ever. My being allowed to come is her thank you.

The basement's already set up by the time I'm home from school.

"Floor pillows?" I say. "Really?"

"Don't make me change my mind, Jericho." Ever's standing next to the bar pouring herself a glass of water. "If you wanna help, go get the door. One of your friends just messaged and said they're outside."

By 4:15, everyone's sitting cross-legged in a circle trying their best to act normal. Trish looks the closest to comfortable. She's the first person I invited and the first one to say yes. We've been in at least one class together since grade nine and sometimes our friend groups cross so we see each other out at house parties. She speaks fluent Mandarin even though she was born in Canada and always does these cool braids with her hair.

Trish's best friend is Chloe, who's sitting right beside her cupping her hands around a glass of water. Her red-rimmed glasses hide the greenest eyes I've ever seen, and when she speaks, all I can think about are violin strings playing in the background. James also showed up, which I'm happy about. He walked in at the same time as one of Ever or Candace's friends. Lindsay I think. Mark rounds out the bunch. We've known each other since sixth grade when he moved from Toronto out here to Oakville. Candace and Ever know him too, and actually asked him to come the first time. For whatever reason, he showed up this time, although he looks the most nervous. His knee hasn't stopped shaking since he sat down and he hasn't looked at anyone.

Ever's holding a silver, metal ball in her hand that's a bit smaller than a tennis ball.

"I'm happy all of you made it out. I know you must be wondering what's going on and I'm not even sure I have the best explanation."

Candace is listening to Ever, but I catch her scanning everyone's faces.

"The thing is," Ever continues, "we're all here because we're dealing with something fucked up in our lives. Or maybe we're not dealing with it. And maybe that's what this is for; helping us all find a way to deal. But, um ... I think if we just share our stories, then we can at least all feel connected in some way. And I think connection is important. And screaming is important. So let it loose and know that we're all here with you."

Everyone's head is turned in Ever's direction.

"So I guess we'll get started. Whoever has this ball tells their story." Ever turns and hands the ball to Candace.

"Why don't you start?"

Candace doesn't look surprised. She takes the metal ball and places it on her kilt.

"OK. Here goes. Well, I'm Candace. Everyone probably knows that. I'm also adopted, which I'm not sure everyone knows. Not like it's a bad thing. It's probably the best thing that's happened to me in my life. The only shitty part is that I still remember my fake mom."

A few nervous giggles cut through the room.

"I mean I still remember the day she left because she literally left me in my room when I was, like, five. It took two days before Mom, my real mom, came to find me. So yeah, that happened, and I've been dealing with it pretty good till she popped back up last year."

It was Ever's idea to dim the lights. I thought some music in the background would be cool and we decided on lo-fi hip-hop. The only light that's turned up is coming from the center of the room where we're all sitting. It makes it look like there's a spotlight on whoever's talking.

"It's funny because last year was when I got my first tattoo. It was the first real argument my mom and I ever had. When I say real, I mean door slamming, loud screaming, I hate you kind of argument. My mom thinks I'm too young to permanently scar my body like that. I told her it's not a scar, it's art. She didn't like that very much and we went at it for a few days.

"But I love that tattoo. To this day, it's the only one I have. And it's not like it's a bullshit tattoo. There's some real meaning behind it. At least for me."

Candace shows everyone the inside of her forearm. The letters are in Farsi or Arabic. I can never remember which.

"It says *And this too shall pass.* That's the loose English interpretation, but what I take from it is that we should enjoy all the great moments and not get too down when the bad times come, because nothing is forever. Whether it's happy times or not, those moments will all pass. Pretty heavy stuff when you think about it, and I thought about it a lot, which is why I tattooed it on my body. And there's a reason I did it in Persian, but that's another story."

Persian. That's what I meant to say.

"It also gave me some perspective on the bad times. The times I wish never happened and wanted to forget. Queue my fake mom."

"What's her name?" Chloe's voice is so soft that it sounds like a whisper. "Your fake mom, what's her real name?"

Candace's face goes blank. I've never asked her what her fake mom's name is. I'm not sure Ever has, either. The way she looks right now, I'm not sure anyone's ever asked her that question.

"Julia. Her name is Julia Maria Johnson Guzman. She hated when I called her Mom so I called her by her first name since I could talk."

"Damn," James says. "That really sucks."

"I know!" Candace continues. She's holding the ball now and rolling it back and forth in both hands. "That's why I want to clap for this woman. I want to give her a round of applause because she has some fucking nerve trying to walk back into my life.

"I didn't even let her set a foot in our door before I went at her. I really let her have it. But wait. Wait, wait, wait. There's so much that happened before my fake mom showed up at our door. It started with my real mom. She's the one that's behind all this. She's the one who actually kept in contact with my fake ass mother all these years. Not all these years, but enough for me to be pissed about it when she finally told me."

Ever's eyes are stuck to Candace like it's the first time she's heard this story. Trish and Chloe sneak a quick glance at each other. Chloe mouths something I can't make out before they both turn to face Candace again.

"So your real mom was talking to your fake mom?" Chloe asks.

"Yeah."

"And you didn't know about it till she showed up at your door?"

"I knew about it, but not till they'd been talking for more than a year." Chloe nods her head while playing with one of Trish's braids. "That's what I was about to say. I was so pissed at my mom for wasting a single breath on this woman. But I can't say I'm surprised. My mom actually has a heart.

"I cried for days after I found out about them talking. I was mad, but I was really scared too. It's like I didn't trust myself. What if I let her talk to me? What if I gave this woman that I hated one more chance to be a mother?"

"Fuck that," James says. "What kind of parent leaves their kid when they're five and then wants to see them again?" James has a slice of pear in his hand. I nudge his shoulder with my elbow and he gets it.

"Sorry, Candace. It's just bullshit."

"I know," Candace says. "I felt the same way. And I told my mom that there's no way I would ever see my fake mom again. But I also let her know that she could keep talking to her if she wanted to. I told myself that in some backwards kind of way, this is my fake mom's punishment. She gets to hear about how amazing I'm doing and how happy I am without ever getting to see me again.

"But now it's my turn to call bullshit on myself. I knew what would happen. I knew days would pass by and I'd still be pissed, then weeks would go by and I'd be a little less pissed. Then that anger would eventually turn to curiosity. And once I was curious, all those walls would come tumbling down in a fraction of the time it took me to build them all up.

"It didn't even take that long. After a couple of weeks, I was already asking my mom if she spoke to my fake mom that day."

*"What did she say?"*

*"What did you tell her?"*

*"How does she sound?"*

"And then that day came. My fake mom was at our house and I was blasting her before she even had a chance to take off her flats."

"You actually agreed to see her?" That's Trish. Her face is usually pretty stoic, but right now it looks like she's watching that *Game of Thrones* episode where they kill everyone at the wedding.

"Yeah, I did," Candace says.

"Why?" That's Mark. I almost forgot he was even here. His knees aren't shaking anymore, but he still barely looks up from under his Raptors cap. "Why would you agree to see her if you hated her so much?"

Candace is staring down at the silver ball that she's cupping in one hand before covering it with the other. The circle feels heavy now. The lo-fi music is so low you can hear Candace's bracelets ping when her hand shifts.

"You don't have to do this," Ever says to Candace. She stands up and looks around the room. "None of you have to do this if you don't want to. We're all just here to talk without worrying about anyone screenshotting our texts. That's why I wanted to do this in person. No one's gonna use any of this against you. Once you leave here, it's all just a memory, or like a lucid group dream or something."

"Like an orgie without the sex." For once, one of James' crude jokes actually helps to break the tension instead of start some shit. Ever's shaking her head but smiling and Candace isn't staring at her hands anymore.

"I'm fine," Candace says. "I wanna keep going."

Ever gives her a look and Candace nods her head. She sets the silver ball back down on her kilt and picks up where she left off.

"To answer your question, I don't know why I agreed to see her. Because you're right, I did hate her. I think I still do. But, I don't know, whatever that thing is between a birth mother and their child probably took over. I just wanted to see her even though I knew I didn't care."

"So what happened after you told her off at the door?" Chloe asks.

"I kept going. I just let her have it till I got everything out. I think the next thing I said after the door was something like, '*Tell me right now that you remember everything you did to me. Every heartless thing you ever said to me when I was barely able to talk. I remember all of it. All of it!*'

"Then she finally got a word in.

"'*Candace.*'

"That's the first thing she said. Real calm too, with that fucking voice I haven't heard since I was coloring outside the lines. A face that was all of a sudden filled with all these emotions of misery and sadness and regret and pride behind those moles that were like tiny reminders of all the bad shit she did to me. It's like just hearing her say my name triggered me some more. I told her not to speak to me, not to look at me, just don't do anything.

"I was in my dad's arms before I said another word. I just couldn't stop crying. My mom walked my fake mom to the living room and handed her a glass of water. She was crying too. Slowly, though. It's like her tears were old and taking their time coming down her face. It was the first time in my life I realized how much alike we looked.

"Then I sat on the floor. My mom and dad sat on the couch to either side of me and my fake mom sat by herself on the loveseat. She was wearing this loose, purple dress that touched the floor and her hair was covered in a white headwrap. No one said anything. Mom sat up and put her arms on my shoulder, but still couldn't find the right words.

"*You look so beautiful.*"

"That's the next thing my fake mom finally said. She kinda whispered it, like it was some secret she didn't want anyone else in the room to hear."

"At least she got one thing right," Ever says. Ever hates hearing this story. She hates hearing anything about Candace's fake mom. On the day that this whole thing went down, Candace came straight to our house after and stayed up with Ever all night talking about it. Ever was still grumbling at breakfast the next morning, saying if she ever saw Candace's fake mom in the street, she'd accidentally nudge her in front of oncoming traffic. Candace was still there eating a late breakfast with us and thought Ever was joking. But I was sitting across from Ever at the table and saw her face. Let's just say Candace's fake mom was lucky she was gone.

"Did she bring you a gift?" Mark asks. His voice sounds shaky, like if he's questioning every word he's saying. Candace looks a little surprised.

"Umm, yeah, she did, actually. How did you know?"

"Because every time my mom lets my dad come back, he always brings a gift. It's like he has to buy his way back in."

"Every time?" James asks. "How many times did he leave?"

"I don't know. Three, maybe four times. Usually not longer than a month or something. Just long enough for him to remember that he has a family. Till one time he didn't come back."

"Damn, guess we're all fucked up in here," James says. No one laughs this time. We all look at each other like we just figured out why we're here.

"That's the point," Ever says. "We're all going through shit. Real shit. And we get to scream about it here as loud as we want."

"Fuck yeah!" I know James is high. I know because he's always high. It's just a matter of what he's high on.

"What did she bring you?" It's the first time Lindsay's said anything. Her hair's tied up in a messy bun that she's had to fix two or three times since we've sat down.

"Books," Candace says. "Like old poetry books. William Words-worth and Coleridge, then some twentieth-century stuff like Langston Hughes and George Elliot Clarke. She said she met Clarke and he signed her copy."

"And you kept them, right?" Mark asks. He's turned his Raptors hat to the back and some of his hair is falling out the sides.

"They're all in my room," Candace says. "I wrapped them up in an old T-shirt and left it under my bed."

"I kept all the gifts my dad brought back too," Mark says. "A bike, video games, Raptors gear. I kept all of it even though I know he's never coming back. Or maybe it's because I know he isn't coming back. He was a dirtbag anyway so Mom is better off without him."

"What about you?" Ever's looking at Mark who's sitting directly across from her. "Are you better off without your father?"

Mark puts his head back down and flips his cap back to the front. Ever's still staring, waiting for an answer. And I know that look. As much as Ever says that we only have to share what we're comfortable with, when there's something she wants to know, you better spit it out. Nothing else is happening till she knows. Mark's about to find that out because when he looks up, Ever's face hasn't moved or changed expressions.

"I don't know. He's my dad. What can I say?"

Ever's cup of water is almost empty. "I don't know what's worse, my dad being dead or yours being alive. Neither of them are coming back home."

"I guess you're right," Mark says. I can't really tell if Mark means it or if he's over talking about his dad. By the time Candace finishes her story paired with the chatter in between and after, over an hour passes. But I'm pretty sure this is what Ever wants. She wants everyone getting deep into their feelings.

"You think you're ever gonna see her again?" We're all standing around in different spots of the basement. Candace and I are sitting on the staircase leading upstairs when Mark asks Candace that question.

"I don't want to," Candace says. "But I have a feeling that wasn't the last time we'll be seeing each other."

James is last to leave. When I turn around from shutting the door, Ever and Candace are hugging it out at the top of the basement staircase.

"You guys all done?" Mom asks. She's in the kitchen with a green smoothie in her hand and her favorite shawl thrown carefully over one shoulder.

"Yes, we are," Ever says. She's still holding on to Candace's arm.

"And? How did it go?" Ever looks at Candace then looks over at me. "OK," Mom says. "How about I pour everyone a glass of wine, one glass, and you tell me all about it in the living room?"

"That sounds great, Cy," Candace says. "But I gotta go. There's this fashion webinar I wanna catch, but next time for sure." Candace and Ever hug one more time before she's out the door. Three hours later and Mom, Ever, and I are still on the couch. Ever's on her fourth glass of wine and I don't even know how many Mom drank. I still haven't finished my first.

"Do you remember the first time you were drunk?" Mom says to Ever, who's lying on her lap with the glass in her hand. "Or I should say the first time I knew you were drunk?"

"Oh God," Ever says. "How can I forget? It was my fourteenth birthday."

"You let Ever drink when she was fourteen?" I ask. "Where was I?"

"I didn't let Ever do anything. You were away somewhere with James, I think. We had a few of Ever's friends over and they were having a good time in the basement. Little did your dad and I know that everyone was having too good a time."

"One of the boys brought a small bottle of whisky he took from his house," Ever says. "I thought he was passing it around to everyone, but apparently it was just me and him. I must've taken five or six shots of that thing."

"When the party was over and everyone left, your father and I couldn't find Ever," Mom says. "It was only about ten o'clock so we didn't think Ever would be in bed, but when we finally checked her room, there she was, lying on her stomach with a bucket on the floor."

"I still don't know where I found that bucket."

"We don't either," Mom says. "None of us remember ever buying that thing. Your dad was so upset, he called every single parent and made them ask their kid if they were the culprit."

Mom is absently stroking Ever's hair. The laughter that's filled the last few hours fades into a familiar silence that only happens when we talk about Dad. Ever's wine glass is on the floor. Mom is swirling her glass and staring past me.

"Do you ever think that our life is better without Dad?" Ever asks.

"What?" I thought I heard Ever wrong. "What do you mean better without Dad?"

"I wasn't talking to you, I was talking to Mom."

"Well, we're both sitting right here so I'm gonna answer. And I think I can speak for Mom when I say that that's the dumbest shit you've ever said."

"Don't speak to your sister like that, Jericho."

Ever's sitting up now and I'm standing.

"It's OK, Mom. Little Jericho is just in his feelings right now."

"In my feelings? Shouldn't you be in your feelings? Our dad is dead and you're asking if our life is better without him in it?"

"You don't know shit, Jericho. So why don't you sit back down and chill the fuck out or run away to your room or something."

"Enough!" It's so odd to hear Mom raise her voice. Ever must be thinking the same thing because she actually stops.

"Ever, no, I do not think our lives are better or could ever be better without your father. Why would you ask me that?"

"It's just a question, Mom. I don't know. It was a thought in my head so I asked it."

"Well, you don't need to have those thoughts. Your father was as close to perfect as they come. I miss him every minute of every day."

I give Ever my best I told you so face and walk up to my room. She and Mom stay down there for at least another hour. Hopefully, they're not drinking anymore wine. That was probably a bad idea. Bad enough to make Ever ask questions that don't make any sense. I want to text Candace, but I'm not really in the mood to talk about anything. I put my headphones on and let *To Pimp a Butterfly* take me away.

# CANDACE

I'M STARING AT EVER again. She's sitting on the stool at the island in her kitchen while her chef sprinkles seasoning on what's about to be another incredible seafood dish. I'm sitting beside her with my elbow up on the island leaning my face on my hand. Ever's hair is twisted into two long braids, one of them resting near the bottom of her back, the other curled near her lap. It's the middle of spring so her skin hasn't hit that summer glow yet, but watching her flip the pages still makes me feel like I'm inside of an Egyptian pyramid watching Isis reading a scroll.

Her phone is on the island too, and after every few pages, Ever checks a message without responding. I know the messages are from our BAGS group because I'm getting them too. I still can't get over our group name. *Boys and Girls Screaming*. I wonder how long it took Ever to come up with it. Shortening it to BAGS makes sense but doesn't do it justice, especially when James texts shit like "Hello teabaggers" with a row of cucumbers.

Doesn't matter though. We haven't stopped getting messages in our group since after the first session. First, it was just a bunch of thank yous to Ever, now everyone wants to know when the next meetup is. It's the weekend so we're both sort of functioning in slow motion, but Ever doesn't want to waste any time in setting up the next session.

"What do you think about having our next BAGS session this week?"

"I think we can do it, but do you think it's too soon, though?"

"Nope. Therapy is like a once-a-week thing and I keep telling you that this is our therapy."

"OK. I'm up for it. Let's do it."

Ever finally looks up from her book and gives me a small smile. She's quiet again after that. The chef lifts the pot off the stove and flips some shrimp in the air. His apron barely has any stains on it even though I see at least two different sauces.

"I think we should get Lindsay to talk next," Ever says. "She was kinda quiet last time."

"Yeah, she's always kinda quiet in class too. But you're right. Let's see if she'll open up."

Chef puts a bowl of blueberries on the table and lets us know dinner will be ready in a few minutes.

"If we manage to get through Lindsay, I think I'm gonna talk next," Ever says.

"You should. I think everyone's kinda curious about how you're dealing with your stuff."

"I think I'm curious about how I'm dealing with my stuff."

That night, I dream about riding horses with my dad. I've had this dream before, or something close to it. We're just riding and riding and it's like we're on a Ferris wheel because everything around me feels like it's spinning. And I look at my dad and he's looking at me and just like that, I'm back at Ever's house, in her bedroom. She's not here, but there's someone curled up on the floor beside the window with their head between their legs. I can't make out who it is, but I know I know who they are. Every step I take forward pulls me further away from the person and now I'm reaching out my hand to grab them and they finally reach out their hand to grab me and boom, I wake up. Same place every time. I have no idea what that dream means and I really don't care. Every time it happens, though, I wake up sweating like I ran 10k in the middle of July so I always wish I never have that dream again.

It's already the day of the BAGS session. Everyone's sitting in the same spot they did last time, except for Ever who hasn't sat down yet at all. James seems a bit tamer this week. Last week I swear he was hopped up on something. Mark's wearing the same Raptors cap and Jericho's looking cute as fuck with his school shirt untucked and that new gold chain he just bought. We're definitely going back to my place after this is over.

Ever finally sits with her legs crossed and the silver ball in her lap. Cups of water are in front of everyone else.

"Candace and Mark got us going last week," she says. "I was thinking this week..."

"Can I go?" Lindsay puts her hand up like we're actually in class. "It's just, if I don't go today, I'll probably never say anything."

"I was gonna suggest you start anyway so go ahead." We pass the silver ball around till it gets to Lindsay, who closes her eyes and takes a deep breath.

"All right. OK. So." Lindsay still hasn't opened her eyes and her face is starting to turn red. "So, umm, a few years ago. No, that's not true. Last year is when this happened. You know how that first trip to the cottage after the winter is the worst. You're basically just cleaning the whole time and don't really get to enjoy anything."

All of us know what that's like. Ever and I are the queens of getting out of that first trip.

"Obviously I was tryna get out of it and made up some excuse. Basically, everyone went, even my two older sisters, and I was home alone for the weekend. I didn't really have anything planned so I invited my boyfriend over. I should say my ex-boyfriend."

"You mean Cal?" Trish asks.

"Yeah. Him. He came over and brought one of his friends and we're just drinking and doing regular stuff. But then he gets all weird and asks me if I wanna do a threesome and I tell him 'fuck no,' especially not with his sketchy-looking friend."

I know that none of the stories anyone of us tells is supposed to have a happy ending, but for this one, I want to cover both my ears like I'm a toddler in front of grownups.

"And at first he's cool and doesn't really push it, but we keep drinking and do some other stuff and we start making out. Then his friend tries to touch my leg and I push his hand away and Cal tells me not to worry. To just let it happen."

"Let it happen?" I blurt out. "What the fuck does that even mean?"

"I don't know, but he kept trying to touch me and then Cal stops making out with me and tells me I should kiss his friend. And I ask him if I kiss him will he get off the couch and Cal says yeah just one kiss."

I know what all the girls are thinking right now. I'm wondering about what's going through the boys' heads.

"And I was already kinda drunk so I just kissed him. Then he comes on top of me and starts kissing my neck and tries taking off my top and the whole time Cal is just watching. He's just sitting there on the couch watching this happen. And then I finally push his friend off me and tell him to get out and Cal just laughs and tells me I'm being uptight. He actually said that word. So I tell him he needs to get the fuck out too. And ... and ...

Linday's in tears before she can get the rest out. Chloe lets her dip her head into her shirt and tells her it's OK. Ever looks uncomfortable, like she's never heard anything like this in her life. But she has. All the girls in here have.

"Did anything ever happen?" Jericho asks. "I mean did you tell your mom or the cops or something?" Lindsay is still in tears when she lifts her head from Chloe's shirt.

"I haven't told anyone and I don't want anyone to know."

"Can we at least fuck Cal up?" James really is an idiot sometimes, even though I know he's not trying to be. When Lindsay finally seems like she's found her composure, Ever asks her if she's dated anyone since.

"Yeah, I'm dating someone now. It's only been a month, but it's the first boy I've dated since Cal. We haven't done anything more than kiss, though. Even though sometimes I want to, something just feels weird. It's like my body has an allergic reaction to the thought of sex."

"That sucks," Chloe says. "Maybe you should try thinking of having sex with other girls." Everyone glares in Chloe's direction.

"What?" she says. "Don't act like none of you have thought about it." It's just the kind of comment to cut some of the emotions in the room. I take the opportunity to grab the ball from Lindsay and toss it over to Ever.

"Your turn."

Everyone's back at attention. Ever's cross-legged rolling the silver ball back and forth on the floor in front of her.

"My dad's dead. I guess everyone knows that. He died of a heart attack or complications from a heart attack or something like that. Doesn't really matter because he's never coming back."

It's crazy that with all the space in this basement, it still feels like the walls are too close.

"I mean, that was impossible to deal with and then my mom had a stroke and couldn't even walk for months. It's like the universe was giving me the middle finger. It felt unbearable for a long time. And the thing is, I don't know, this might sound weird, but the thing is that I think I took my mom getting sick worse than I did my dad dying."

"What do you mean?" Trish says. "At least your mom's still here. You just said it sucks because your dad is never coming back but your mom is, like, upstairs or something."

"I know, I know. It doesn't always make sense to me either. But my mom was like a butterfly before the stroke. She was this beautiful butterfly just floating around the world who everyone kind of admired. Most insects or whatever are disgusting. You slap them away if they ever try to land on you. But butterflies, you want to touch them. You want them to land on your stomach and feel their wings. After the stroke, it's like my mom became stuck in this cocoon. And I know what's in there. I know there's this beautiful thing inside trying to get out, but it can't."

"Does your mom know you feel like this?" Lindsay asks.

"Yeah, does Mom know you feel like this?" Jericho says. Ever's told him how she feels about their mom before so I know Jericho's just being annoying.

"Why are you even talking?" Ever snaps back.

Jericho lifts both his arms to show he's backing off. Ever's told me this a million times before so it's not so shocking for me. I give Jericho a chill the fuck out stare and he seems to get it.

"Keep going, Ever," I say. "No one's judging you."

"Maybe someone else should go today. I don't know if I'm ready. There's just stuff that no one knows and I don't ... I don't know."

"But we're here to talk about the stuff that no one knows about," Mark says. "Boys and girls screaming, remember?"

I know what Ever's thinking. I know she wants to get up right now and run upstairs and slam her door. She's weighing out the consequences in her mind right now. She started this thing and now she has to own it.

"You just hate seeing her as anything less than amazing, right?" James' braids are hanging over the front of his face when he talks and it's hard to tell who he's looking at. "It's like your parents are supposed to be special. They're supposed to be the one thing in your life that makes sense. And when they don't, it's like living on a minefield or something. One wrong step and shit blows the fuck up."

I don't think any of us has ever heard James string together that many coherent words without making some kind of joke or straight up disrespectful comment. Jericho only brings him over to my place once in a while so it's not like we've had many conversations, but even Jericho looks surprised right now.

"Yeah, it is kinda like that," Ever says. "But no matter what, I always feel ..."

"Guilty?" James swipes his braids and you can finally see his entire face. "Guilty because you think you should be able to do something to fix it. Or sometimes you feel like you're the cause of it."

"How are you in my head like this?" Ever says.

"Because I know how you feel. Except my stepmom isn't a butterfly. She's a fucking monster."

Ever rolls the silver ball over to James who grabs it and tosses it in the air before catching it again.

"Guess I'm up," James says. "Maybe I shouldn't even be blaming my stepmom. Maybe I should be blaming my dad for letting my real mom go. For being such a fucking asshole that my mom didn't want anything to do with either of us. He's the real culprit."

"Where's your real mom?" Lindsay asks. "Don't you visit her or doesn't she come visit you?"

"I don't know where she is. She used to call once in a while, but never visited. Last time I saw her I was twelve."

I think Jericho's told me some of this stuff about James before but I don't really remember. Hearing it from James, though, sounds like a whole new story.

"Maybe I'm the monster, though. It's not like I ever gave my stepmom a real chance. I don't even try to pretend I like her, and I guess pretending isn't her thing either. So every time I'm home, it's like ... I don't know, I guess it's like, how do you leave your kid? That's all I can think about when I'm at home. How does a mom just say fuck it and run away without really looking back?"

"If you find out, let me know," I say.

Ever doesn't even crack a smile at that one even though everyone else chuckles.

"So what do you do about feeling guilty?" Ever asks James.

"Drugs," he says. James pulls out a bag of weed and another bag of pills and dangles them in the air. "Never leave home without it."

That gets Ever to crack a smile and everyone else follows. Just like that, we're all belly laughing and shaking our heads at the same time.

"I've never tried any pills before," Ever says. "What kind are those?"

"The kind you shouldn't try on your first time," James says.

"Does it help," Ever asks.

"Nothing helps. But it feels really fucking good sometimes."

Out of nowhere, the lo-fi changes up and some trap beats start playing through the basement speakers. It almost scares me till I realize it's Jericho syncing music on his phone. A Migos song, of course, and he's bopping his head and mouthing the lyrics.

"I think we need a break," Jericho says. "Our chef made some appetizers we were saving for afterwards and I can grab a bottle of tequila from the bar."

"Sounds good to me," Trish says.

Chloe's nodding her head. "Sounds good to me too," she says.

Jericho's already choosing a bottle. Ever and I look at each other and shrug our shoulders.

"Break time!" We say simultaneously. I head over to the bar, and Ever runs upstairs to grab the appetizers. By the time she gets back down, we all have shot glasses in our hands and I give Ever hers.

"Make a toast, Ever," I say. "You're the reason we're all here."

"There's only one thing to toast," she says.

"Boys and Girls Screaming." We all shout it together and tap our glasses. Two more shots in and the music sounds louder now. Trish and Chloe are keeping us entertained with their dance moves. Ever just downed another shot and is headed for more.

"You're going kinda hard, aren't you?" I say. "You're gonna be jumping on top of tables soon if you don't slow down."

"I'm good," Ever says. "I think we've partied harder than this plenty of times."

"Are we partying though?"

Ever's already ignoring me and making her way over to James, who's tossing another piece of prosciutto in his mouth.

"Let me try one of those," Ever says.

"One of what?"

"Don't be slow, James. You know what I'm talking about. Let me try one."

James looks over at Jericho who's standing close enough to him to hear what's going on.

"You wanna do this right now?" Jericho asks Ever. "Trust me, once you take one, there's no turning back."

James is reaching in his back pocket, but I can tell he doesn't really want to do it. Ever knows it too, so she reaches around and plucks the bag from James' pocket, throws two pills in her mouth and takes it back with a shot of tequila.

"OK, so I guess we're doing this," James says. He pops one then hands one out to everyone else. Mark and I are the only ones who refuse. I also haven't seen Mark take any other drink since our first shot.

Another hour passes and it's getting dark outside. Ever hasn't slowed down and neither has anyone else. Jericho's in the corner talking to Lindsay and I'm grinding my teeth every time she smiles and twirls her hair. James is right beside him speaking to Chloe and Trish and they're all sipping a pineapple, cranberry juice and tequila mix that Ever made a few minutes ago.

"Where's your drink, sis?" Ever's eyes are barely open. She has a drink in her hand and is swaying back and forth like we're listening to the final song at Coachella.

"I'm good," I say. "And you look like you're good too. You better hope Cy doesn't decide to come down here and see you like this."

"Cy? You mean my mother? Don't worry about her. She's probably meditating or something."

I take Ever's drink away from her and grab onto her hand.

"Hey, why don't you come sit down over here for a bit?"

"Sit down? We're partying. Why do you want me to sit down?" Ever pulls her hand away from me and tries to turn around. Before she can take another step, she falls to the ground.

"Ever!" I'm on the floor beside her right away, holding her head in both my arms. "Ever. Wake up, Ever." Jericho's next on the floor beside me. He's tapping Ever's face telling her to open her eyes. Now everyone's crowding around. The music's still going and it's hard to think straight.

"Ever!" She's not completely unconscious, or at least I don't think she is. James fills a cup with water from the bathroom and splashes it on Ever's face. When she doesn't even flinch, I could feel sweat curl up at the back of my neck.

"We have to call an ambulance," I say. "Jericho! Call a fucking ambulance right now."

I'm still holding Ever's head up. "Go tell Cy what's happening. And turn off this goddamn music."

## CANDACE

THIS DREAM WON'T END. I thought I've woken up twice already only to be sucked back into a stream of images I'm trying to run away from. I don't even know if my eyes are closed. I see stains on the wall in front of me. Green and red and purple colors splashed all over the walls. No matter how hard I scrub against the wall, the colors just won't come off. I'm trying to move my arms faster but they feel stuck. When I open my mouth to scream, I'm transported back to my room. Or a version of my room. Shadows are bobbing like they would in a late evening campfire. Some of the shadows I can make out. They can see me too.

When I wake up for real, Ever's eyes are still closed. She has two pillows under the side of her face and the bed is inclined just enough so she's not completely flat. There's only one IV stuck at the top of her forearm this morning. The day after the doctors pumped her stomach, I didn't even want to count.

It feels too quiet in here. I put my ear to Ever's mouth to make sure she's breathing, something I've done at least two dozen times since she's been here. I take a moment to stretch my back out now that I'm up and pull a thin blanket up close to Ever's shoulders. Her breakfast tray isn't here yet, which means it's still early. Cy's still asleep on the other metal chair, her mouth slightly opened just like her daughter's.

Her daughter. My sister. How could I let this happen? I knew Ever wasn't right before she took that first shot. She struggled to share her story and when she took those pills, I should've ended the session right there. The only thing I'm happy about is that she's alive. I don't know what I would've done if things were worse. Thank God we got her here when we did. Once Jericho came back downstairs with Cy, I knew things would be OK. She got us to lift Ever onto the couch and pressed her fist into the top of Ever's stomach. Ever made a weird kind of sound and then Cy told us to flip her onto her side. It couldn't have been more than five minutes before the ambulance got there. Cy rode with Ever. Jericho and I hopped in an Uber after we sent everyone home.

Doctors said Ever was lucky. They've seen worse results with fewer drugs and alcohol in the system. I don't feel any kind of luck. When they finally said that Ever would be OK, that she'd just have to stay here for a few days to run some tests and recover a little bit, the only thing I wanted to do was hide in the closet. The thought of explaining to Cy how Ever ended up in the hospital made me nauseous.

"I'm sorry, Cy." It was all I could get out once we were finally alone in the waiting room. "I don't know when it got out of control. We were just drinking and Ever just kept going and by the time I tried to take her drink away from her it was too late."

Cy lifted her arm and let me cry on her lap.

"It's OK, Candace. Doctors said she's going to be fine." Cy was stroking my hair and speaking so softly I barely heard her. There were tears in her eyes too, and despite how calm she was I knew she was disappointed in me.

"Why would Ever take drugs," Cy asked. There were strangers two or three seats removed from our seat and Cy's voice stayed in almost a whisper. "I know she drinks, I even know you guys go for weed walks, but why hard drugs?"

"I don't know," I said. "She's never done anything like that before. It was strange. She was talking about her dad dying then talking about your stroke, but it was hard for her to get out her feelings. Then when we took a break, she just took it to another level."

My mom got there before we had a chance to finish that conversation. I've only left the hospital to shower and change since then. No way I'm leaving my sister until she walks out of here with me. The nurse gives a polite knock on the door and pushes in a tray of food. Cy wakes up at the sound of the knock, but Ever's still sound asleep.

"Time to eat some breakfast, honey." The nurse ignores us and gently shakes Ever's leg. I catch a touch of Jamaican accent which reminds me of my fake mom. Ever opens her eyes and the nurse raises the back of her bed and puts the tray on Ever's lap.

"Hopefully, this is the last meal you'll be eating in here," the nurse says. "You'll probably be discharged before lunch. But eat up. I'll be back in a bit to check your IV."

The nurse smiles at me and Cy before letting the door close behind her. Ever's smiling too, but the bags under her eyes and the fact that her skin looks like she's been bitten by a vampire tells a different story.

"You're still here?" Ever says.

"Where else would I be?"

"Home. In a real bed. Where I wish I was right now."

Ever let Cy do her hair in a single French braid the first morning we were here. Two days later and it's still intact.

"You need to relax," Cy says. She's taking the knife and fork on Ever's tray out of the package. "The nurse just said you'll be home in a few hours. You just need to take it easy and eat this prison food till then."

I don't know how Cy's doing this. The sight of Ever in a hospital gown on a hospital bed with a needle injected into her forearm in a room that smells like the flu sinks my heart every time. But Cy, she's still finding ways to make this sterile room feel like there's something more in here. It's her gift. I really can't think of a time since after that all-white party when Cy has been anything but positive. Does Ever realize that? She's been so stuck on ways Cy hasn't been herself that maybe she's missing it. I'm going to make sure to tell her that once she's out of here.

"Chef said he's making your favourite dish when you get home," Cy says.

"Scallops?" It's the most energy Ever's showed since getting rolled in here.

"With calamari and another surprise I'm not telling you."

Ever drinks the cup of orange juice, but still doesn't touch the food. Cy's still standing beside her and I can feel what's coming next. I know Ever feels it too because she sits up on her bed and raises the incline like its extra support.

"And after you're done eating your welcome home meal, we need to talk. We really need to talk. You have to help me understand how you got yourself in here because I can't figure it out."

Ever looks at me, but doesn't say anything. Even though I explained everything to Cy, there's no way she's not hearing every single detail directly from Ever herself. Ever nods at her mom who smiles back before sitting down again.

I think of all the things I want to ask Ever too. All the things I want to know and even some things I probably don't. I'm still trying to decide if I'm surprised that this happened. That this is where Ever would end up. Sitting in this hospital has given me time to relive all of the questionable stuff that Ever said. In some ways it's so obvious. Her father died. That's more than enough reason right there, but Ever's been functioning normally for years since then. At least I think she has. I know her mom's stroke has been messing with her a lot, but enough for her to lose herself like that? And why now? Did the BAGS really stir up that many repressed emotions?

It feels like something's off. I know Ever doesn't do anything by accident. You're talking about someone who used to plan out her outfits for the week in grade two. So if Ever's in the hospital, it's because she wanted to be here. As backwards as that sounds, the more I think about it, the more I believe it's true.

The BAGS have been messaging nonstop since that night. I've been messaging back updates so they know Ever's fine. I'll probably let them know she's coming home today. I know James will be relieved. He's been DMing me the most telling me how bad he feels that he let Ever take those pills. I tell him it's not his fault even though I'm sure he feels the exact opposite. And if there's anyone to blame it's me for letting that evening play out the way it did. We should've stuck to our rules, which is no drinking or anything else till after our sessions are over. Ever made that rule up herself because she knew alcohol and emotions are a bad mix.

We totally fucked that one up and look where we are. Actually, I'm wondering where we take the BAGS from here. We can't continue without Ever, but will Ever still want to do it? I haven't spoken to her about it. I really haven't spoken to her about anything and don't plan to till she's back home and feeling like herself again. But I also don't want the BAGS to be over. I know how much Ever wanted this and to be honest, it felt good sharing my stuff with the group. Even though we've only met up a couple of times, we already feel like a unit. We message each other every day in between our sessions talking about stuff that has nothing to do with trauma.

*Emergency meeting.* I post that in our group chat.

*Wait, not emergency. Ever's fine. I mean urgent meeting. Can you guys meet in Ever's basement right now?*

It's Sunday so I expect everyone to say yes. Plus, Jericho's been home because Cy doesn't let him sleep in the hospital. Less than a minute and everyone replies with some emoji that lets me know that they can make it.

"I'm gonna take off," I say to Cy and Ever. "I need to shower and eat some real food. But I'll be at your place by the time you get home. I'm not missing those scallops."

I kiss Ever on the cheek and give Cy a hug and jump in an Uber straight for Ever's. Jericho's waiting at the door when I pull up.

"Trish and Chloe are already here."

"Good," I say. Mark is walking up the driveway at the same time Lindsay pulls up in her SUV.

"Where's James?" I ask Jericho. We're still just outside his front door.

"He texted me a while ago and said he wasn't sure if he should come."

"Tell him get his ass over here, ASAP." James must have heard me because here he comes peddling his bike in the middle of our street. He tosses it on the driveway and walks straight past us into the house.

We all find our spots sitting in the same circle that's starting to become routine. After letting the group know that Ever's coming home soon, it's time to get down to business.

"I think there's more going on with Ever than she's letting on," I say. "I've known her almost all my life and I've never seen her lose control like that."

"What do you think it is?" Chloe asks. "Do you think she has some kind of sickness she doesn't want anyone to know about?"

"No, that's not it," I say.

"I definitely would've known that," Jericho chimes in.

"So what are you thinking?" Lindsay says.

"I don't know, but we need to find out," I say. It's so hard sitting still right now. Being back in this basement that I've played in or eaten in or come down to grab a bottle of something at least a million times now carries a different kind of feeling. I'm sitting in the spot that Ever collapsed. I can feel her dead weight in my arms. There's no way I'm letting that memory cast a shadow on over ten years of friendship, ten years of being my sister.

"Maybe it's some kind of family thing," Mark says.

"What do you mean?" I ask.

"Maybe Ever knows something about her mom or dad. Like maybe she caught one of them cheating or maybe she found out something shady that she's had to keep a secret."

I thought about it and that would make sense. Ever loves her family but loves the idea of family even more. If something were to puncture her impression of what she thought about her family, I could see that weighing her down, especially if she couldn't talk to anyone about it.

"You might not be too far off," Jericho says. "I don't know anything, but I know if there was something, Mom would know and try to carry it on her own. So if Ever did find out, that's who we'd have to talk to."

"But Cy would never tell us anything. Not if it's a secret she's kept for who knows how many years."

"She wouldn't need to tell us if we found out on our own," says Jericho.

"And how would we do that?" James asks. "Search the house for clues?" James has a hood over his braids and both hands in the hoodie's pockets. I'm guessing by the bags under his eyes that he hasn't slept for days, but he's still sharp enough for sarcasm so he must be doing OK.

"Not the whole house," Jericho says. "Just Ever's room."

Me and Jericho look at each other then look at the rest of the group.

"We still have at least two or three hours before Ever and Cy get home. Let's go."

I lead us up the stairs in single file like we're coming back inside during elementary school recess till we're in front of Ever's door.

"Are we sure we want to do this?" I ask. Being at Ever's door with the rest of the BAGS suddenly feels wrong. "It could be nothing, guys. Maybe Ever was just having a bad day."

"And maybe she wasn't." The look on Jericho's face let me know there's no way he's letting this go.

"OK, let's do it."

We walk in and split up to different parts of the room. We're opening and closing drawers, Jericho's on the floor looking under Ever's bed, Trish and Chloe are in her closet while Mark is kind of floating around.

"What are we actually looking for?" Mark asks. "It's not like Ever's gonna write down what she saw."

"Actually, that's exactly what she would do." I can't believe I didn't think of this before we played detective.

"If Ever has any kind of secret, it's gonna be in her journal. And I know where it is."

"So where is it?" Jericho asks. "Grab it so we can find out."

"I can't do that. None of you can read it. I'll read it myself and let you know if I find anything, but there's no way I'm letting everyone read Ever's diary. That's not happening."

Ever's kept a diary since she was ten years old. Every thought that's in her head that she doesn't speak out loud is on those pages. It wasn't long till those pages turned into books. Four at last count, each of them placed in a wooden box Ever's dad made before she got to high school and buried in the backyard. But Ever, being Ever, didn't want to have to dig the box up every time she felt like reminiscing. One winter weekend the year we turned sixteen, Ever took pictures of all the pages of every diary she ever wrote in and saved them on a USB stick. And that USB stick is in a slit at the bottom of her mattress.

"I need to get started right now," I say. "You guys should go. It's probably not a good idea for all of you to be here when Ever gets back. If I find anything, I'll let you know."

I stay in Ever's room and connect the USB to her laptop. Just seeing her writing puts me right back on our elementary school desks, side by side as usual. Even at ten, her printing was precise. It's like she put care into correctly writing out every letter in its exact form. And some of the stories those letters spelled out were full of childish wonder. Ambitions of being a scientist or an architect or some job where she gets to discover things. Admitting to young crushes and summer days spent on the lake with her parents sailing to Toronto for lunch. I didn't even know it was possible to feel nostalgia from your preteen years, but the only thing more interesting than Ever's life is her imagination.

Nothing jumps out in the first book. I'm skimming, but I have a feeling that even though I'm not sure what I'm looking for, whatever it is will jump out of the screen once I see it. That's what I tell myself, anyway. According to these dates, Ever's twelve now. More stories of family vacations, I laugh when I read about how she first got her period and remember the excitement when she describes those random trips with her mom. Cy was the best at just taking us away with no warning. She hasn't been nearly as spontaneous since her stroke. I get annoyed because this is probably one of the changes in Cy that Ever's been talking about that I didn't even notice till this very moment. I hate it when she's right.

Still haven't found anything that could be triggering and it's after lunch now so Ever could be home any minute. I'm scrolling a little faster. She's on one of those random trips with Cy in Niagara Falls, but when I scroll to the next page, it's all scratched out. So is the next page and the one after that. Three pages of stories are scribbled over so that there's no way I can make out anything Ever wrote.

"Jericho." That's Cy calling for Jericho. She just came in the front door which means Ever's home too. I eject the USB as quickly as I can and slide under Ever's bed. The slit was a lot easier to find when I didn't hear footsteps coming up the stairs. I finally feel it with my fingers and slide it back in just in time to open Ever's room door before she does it herself.

"Sis!" I say, and squeeze Ever over both her arms without giving her a chance to hug me back. "I almost forgot what you look like without hospital clothes on."

Ever wiggles out of my arms and flops face-down on her bed.

"I missed you so much," she says to her bed. "I'll never leave you again."

I take that opportunity to close Ever's laptop and sit on the bed beside her.

"How you feeling?" I ask.

"Great," she says, still with her face in the pillow.

"Ever." She hears the tone of my voice and sits up. "Seriously, how are you?"

She looks fine. She has headphones around her neck and Band-Aids on both her arms. Her face could use some color, but if I ate that hospital food for three days I'd look like I wasn't born with melanin too.

"Seriously, I'm good. I actually feel more rested and energized than I have in a long time. So stop looking at me like that and tell me how the meeting went."

"Meeting?"

"Yeah. I saw on the BAGS chat that you guys met up today. I'm guessing I was the topic of conversation. Does everyone think I'm crazy?"

I don't know why I'm so unprepared to answer Ever's question.

Yes, we had a meeting. Yes, the meeting was about her, but how much do I tell? I'm obviously not going to tell her we searched her room like a forensic squad looking for clues, but I need to say something.

"Oh yeah. Um, it was whatever. We just got together to figure out if there was anything we could do to help you once you got home. But then I thought you probably wouldn't wanna see everyone here when you got back from the hospital so I made them leave. Maybe you could send a message in the chat to let everyone know you're all right. Whenever you're up for it, of course."

"That's a good idea," Ever says. "I should do that right now. We should probably plan our next meeting too. What day do you think?" Ever's already typing away on her phone as she's talking to me.

"Hey, slow down a bit. You literally just got back two minutes ago and you're ready to plan another session? I wasn't even sure if you'd wanna keep the group together."

Ever lays her phone down, folds her hands in her lap and takes a deep breath.

"Listen, I don't know what it must've felt like for you to be holding me when I passed out. I know you were scared and probably thought the worst shit was gonna happen. But I'm telling you that I'm good. I'm really good. It took me accidentally overdosing to get here, but I'm actually kinda glad it happened."

"How can you be glad you almost died?"

"Because now I get to live. I actually thought I was dead, Candace. When I fell down I could still hear everything you guys were saying. I heard all the screaming and felt the water on my face and

Jericho running up the stairs. I heard everything in the back of that ambulance all the way till I was on the hospital bed. And when I woke up, I knew I was lucky to be alive."

Ever gets up, walks over to her window and opens the curtain. "My life's not gonna stop because of what happened. I just wanna keep going."

I don't know what else I expected from Ever. She's standing in the center of her window frame looking like a stained-glass image. I'm wondering how she's acting this normal. A few days ago she thought she was going to die and she's ready to link back up with the BAGS again. I don't know if I believe her.

"What happened in Niagara Falls?"

Ever turns away from the window.

"What do you mean what happened in Niagara Falls? What are you talking about?"

I'm already regretting this. Ever said she's fine. She just said she feels great and is happy to be alive. I should've left it at that. But I can't. If there's something Ever's holding on to it can pop up at any time. And who's to say anyone will be there the next time she thinks it's OK to swallow a bunch of pills.

"Don't get mad, but I read your diary."

"You did what?"

Ever walks towards me till she's on the other side of the bed.

"I was worried about you, Ever. I didn't know what else to do. I wanted to know why you went over the edge like that so I could help you."

"I told you only read it if I die. I'm not dead, Candace."

"But you almost were. And I wasn't gonna wait till it happened again to try to get some answers." Ever's still standing and now I am too. The bed between us is starting to feel like an ocean. "You're my sister, Ever. We tell each other everything, but when I went through your journal and saw those pages scratched out, I knew there was something you're holding back."

"I can't believe you. You're the only person in the world I told about my journal and you know I didn't want anyone reading it." Ever turns away again. "Just leave. I don't wanna talk about this."

I've heard Ever say those words a million times to Jericho. I've even heard her say it to her mom and dad. But she's never said those words to me.

"You want me to leave?"

"Yeah, I do. I should probably be resting right now, anyways."

Part of me can't believe Ever's kicking me out of her room. But the other part of me knows that there's a real reason those diary entries are scratched out. When I get back to my own room, I can't sit still. Why would Ever keep anything from me? I don't get it. What could be worse than any of the stories I've told her about myself or my fake mom?

The BAGS are all telling Ever how happy they are she's back. Ever's thanking everyone and apologizing. She was also serious about setting up another session. She's asking the BAGS which day works best and they're going back and forth. A FaceTime from Jericho interrupts all that.

"Why aren't you still here?" he asks. "Thought for sure you'd at least stay for dinner."

"I did too. Ever had a different idea, though." I tell Jericho about what I saw or didn't see in Ever's journal. Then I tell him about how upset she got when I told her I read it.

"Maybe you should've waited a day or two to tell her you basically read her most private thoughts."

"Maybe. But Ever and I are always straight up with each other. Plus, it's not like I was gonna send a copy into TMZ. We wanted to help her and that was the best way. And it turns out that we're right, there is something she doesn't wanna tell anyone."

Jericho goes silent for a minute. He's lying in his room with no shirt on and mumbling "Niagara Falls" to himself trying to make it make sense.

"And you said she was twelve?"

"Yup."

"I can't think of anything," he says.

"You were eleven, Jericho. Ever could've come home with her hair dyed purple and a nose ring and you wouldn't have noticed."

I barely finish my sentence before I hear something clank against our front window facing the driveway. I tell Jericho I'll call him back and rush downstairs in time to catch my mom hustling to the window too. We hear another clank.

"Call me Julia!" Another rock hits our front window. "I'm your mother and you'll do as I say." Another rock. Then another. There's a small pile of stones beside my fake mom that she reaches for in between her outbursts. Mom is looking at me like her worst nightmare is coming true which isn't that far from what's actually happening.

Another rock.

Now neighbors are peeking through their front doors and landscapers have stopped working to get a glimpse of the action.

"Call me Julia!"

Everyone's in shock but me. Mom still hasn't said a word, but I can feel her fear. This is what scared me about ever speaking to this woman again. It doesn't matter that I was only five when she closed that door behind her, I know who she is. I know what's inside of her soul and it's a dark place where even she doesn't want to be. When she came over that day, I knew it wouldn't be the last time we saw each other. I'd be lying if I said I predicted this, but I knew the next time we were face to face wouldn't be as peaceful.

Another rock.

I'm sure a nanny or housewife has called the police by now so I don't have much time.

"Where are you going?" Mom asks. She grabs me by the arm as I try to walk past her.

"I need to talk to her. She won't hurt me, Mom, but I need to go out there. Just call the police and wait here."

My fake mom is wearing an all-white, strapless dress that nearly touches the ground. Her hair is up in a tight bun and she's wearing a full face of makeup. Her nails are done and she's in green flats. I'm approaching her slowly, but I'm not hesitant. When she finally sees me, she puts down the rock that's in her hand and smiles.

"Sweetheart. You came." She crouches down and opens her arms like she expects me to run into her chest and give her a big hug. When I don't move, she stands back up. "What's the matter, sweetheart? You don't want to hug your mother?"

I move closer, but still don't say anything.

"OK," she says. "I know this isn't the best way to get your attention, but I tried calling that woman. I called and called and she didn't answer. For weeks and months she wouldn't answer. And I wanted to see you so badly, sweetheart, so I got all dressed up and came down here myself."

I remember the only other memory I have of my fake mom with red lipstick. I remember because she had music on the entire day. Whitney Houston playing while she was in the shower, SWV while she got dressed. When she came out into the living room, she was wearing a cream-colored dress and dancing and singing the words to every song. She grabbed me and lifted me into the air to dance with her. We swung round and round and when she finally put me down, she kissed my cheek and left the stain of her red lipstick.

"Why are you here?"

My fake mother looks up at the house. My real mother is standing on the porch, which is far enough away that she can't hear our conversation.

"I don't know, Candace. I don't know what I'm doing here."

There are only a few stones left from the pile. My fake mother picks them up and cups them with both hands. She's still staring at my house. Staring at my mother. She doesn't say anything when she turns and starts walking away. I watch her white dress flow behind her. I see her trying to hold her head up high even though tears have already ruined her mascara.

"Mom!" I say it before I could even think. My fake mom turns around and I run to her. She drops the stones and wraps her arms around me and squeezes. I'm squeezing tight too and don't want to let go. She kisses me on the top of my head and whispers "I love you" over and over.

## CANDACE

I'VE SPOKEN TO JULIA every day for three straight weeks. When the cops came that day, Mom told them my fake mom left and that she didn't think she'd be a threat to come back. But really we had brought her inside and told her to stay upstairs until the cops left. She ended up staying for dinner and then went back upstairs to my room and we spoke for another hour. Dad had come home by then and Mom had to fill him in. After some resistance to my fake mom and me being anywhere out of his sight, he calmed down and let us have some alone time.

I guess I'm going to have to stop calling her my fake mom. It's pretty much habit, but now I feel guilty every time I think it. Even though we speak every day, the real conversation happened when Julia left that night. Mom, Dad, and I sat in the living room. They were beside each other on the same couch and I sat on the floor in front of the single-seater.

"Well," Mom said, "that was quite an evening."

"I'd say so," Dad said. "I guess we have a lot to think about."

"Nothing changes for me," I said. "You're my mother. You'll always be my mother. I'm not going anywhere. I just think she needs help."

"That's putting it mildly," Dad said. Mom gives him a look and he shrugs his shoulders.

"Yes, clearly Julia needs some kind of help," Mom said. "But what do you want us to do about it, honey?"

I didn't have an answer. Before that day, I never cared about any-thing Julia needed. She was my fake mother. That's how I thought of her and I never really thought that would change. But something has. Seeing her outside our home like that, throwing rocks up against our windows changed a lot for me, but that didn't mean I knew how to help her.

"I don't think any of us knows how to help her," I said. "So why don't we get her to speak to somebody that does."

"Like a doctor?" Dad asked.

"Yeah, or like a psychologist or something. I'm not exactly sure where to start, but we need to know what's actually wrong with her before we make any kind of decisions."

"What do you mean decisions, honey?" Mom's voice was care-ful. I still wasn't sure how she really felt about everything, but she was letting me lead the way so I kept going.

"Decisions ... you know. Like maybe talking to her more regu-larly or maybe she can eventually come over here once in a while. For dinner or something like that, and only when we're all here."

Mom's expression still hadn't changed, and Dad was watching her just as closely as I was.

"I don't know if that's a good idea, Candace," he said. "Maybe we need to give it a bit more time. Let Julia figure things out on her own."

"Because that's worked for eighteen years, right?" Dad was about to say something but crossed his legs and sat back on the couch.

"I agree with your dad, Candace. She was just outside of our home throwing rocks up against our windows. That's not someone I can trust around our family."

"I know," I said. "And we shouldn't trust her. But maybe if we get her some help, she'll at least have a chance to earn our trust."

Mom was shaking her head. It was a lot, I knew that. I was basically asking her to help someone she thought was a threat. But it wasn't just anyone. And as hard as I knew it was for Mom to swallow, that someone had a huge influence on my life, even if most of it was negative.

"I have a friend she can speak to," Mom finally said. "If Julia is willing to meet with her, we can start there." Dad didn't look impressed, but kept his mouth shut. "But she's not allowed anywhere near you or this house until we know it's safe."

Mom wasn't lying. She arranged for Julia to speak to her psychologist friend and when Julia initially refused, I made it clear that if she wanted to be part of my life, this was the only way. She agreed and has been giving me updates ever since. She even said they're working on prescribing some medication which Dad said he'll pay for.

In those same few weeks, I haven't been back to Ever's. I've texted to see how she's doing, but there aren't any emojis in her answers if she answers at all. But today is also our first BAGS meeting since she's been out of the hospital. It would've happened already, but Cy wasn't having it. At least that's what Jericho told me. Eventually Ever convinced her it's what's best and so here we are.

I'm actually nervous. This is the longest Ever and I have gone without really talking to one another. I know she's pissed, but we've had small blowups before and always get over it before Conan comes on. She's really upset this time, I know, but I miss her so much. She doesn't even know about everything that happened with Julia yet. Jericho says he's told her bits and pieces, but it's not the same. She's not hearing it from her sister.

So even though I'm not sure how she's going to react, I show up about fifteen minutes earlier than our BAGS session is supposed to start. Jericho opens the door and tells me Ever's already downstairs.

"Right on time," Ever says. She's putting appetizers out on the bar before turning around and crossing her arms.

"Am I? I actually think I'm early."

"Early for the session, but right on time for me to give you this."

Ever hands me a box about the size of a cellphone. This girl is too much. I don't even know what's inside and I'm ready to break down and start bawling my eyes out. When I open the box, there's a linked gold necklace with a pendant. The pendant is two small paint brushes crisscrossed and the tip of each paintbrush is diamond.

"Ever!"

"You like it?" Ever takes the necklace away and wraps it around my neck. "Do you remember how much you loved that paintbrush when we first met? I swear you had that thing till you were, like, thirteen."

"I still got it somewhere," I say.

"Of course you do." The necklace falls just above the center of my chest. Ever's lifting the pendant gently. "But there's more. Look inside the box."

I look in the box again and lift what I thought was the bottom. Underneath, there's the USB. I look up at Ever who's looking at me like a boyfriend who just nailed my birthday gift.

"We've been sisters since day one," she says. "You're the only person in the world who should be reading this. You've been my real-life diary for so long it only makes sense you read it."

I still don't know what to say. We rest our heads on each other's shoulders and I try not to cry.

"OK, chill," Ever says. "You're gonna make me mess up my make-up before everyone gets here. And I have a lot to say."

It's not long before all the BAGS are sitting cross-legged in our usual spots, except for Ever, who's up on her knees sitting back on her legs.

"Bet you guys didn't think we'd be back here," she says. "I know for sure you didn't think I'd be back here."

Jericho looks anxious and James has his head down with all his braids covering his face.

"But even though what happened last time was messed up, it made me realize that I'm really not good. I mean I am good, but there's just some stuff I need to get off my chest I think. Stuff I've bottled up a bit too long."

It's strange not knowing at all what Ever's thinking or what she's going to say. We've been in each other's heads since forever. I know every part of her. At least that's what I thought.

"When I was twelve, my mom took me to Niagara Falls. We always took these random road trips where she wouldn't tell me where we're going or let me bring any clothes or anything. She'd just tell me to jump in the car. Candace knows what I'm talking about."

I'm nodding my head and Jericho is playfully shaking his.

"This time it was just me and her, though, and when we first got there, everything was cool. We were sitting outside on a patio eating a veggie burger and fries when my mom ran to the bathroom."

"She left you by yourself?" Jericho asks.

"Yeah, I was twelve, not two. Mom didn't coddle me the same way she coddled you."

"Whatever."

"Anyways, when she was in the bathroom and I was going in on the fries, I looked up and saw my dad. My first instinct was to run to him, but then I noticed there was someone beside him. And not just beside him, but really close to him. Like almost intimately close."

"What?" Jericho says. "What do you mean close? Like another woman?"

"Yes, Jericho. Another woman. And they were smiling and she kissed him on the cheek and then he wrapped his arm around her shoulders."

Jericho looks like he just found out his favorite rapper died. He probably has so many questions, but he's still in "I can't believe this" mode and doesn't say anything.

"That's not all," Ever says. "The woman he was with was holding hands with a kid. He must've been about five or six years old."

"So what does that mean?" Mark says.

"It didn't mean anything at first. He was out of sight before I could even process what was happening. Then Mom came out of the bathroom and I acted like there wasn't anything wrong."

"You didn't tell Mom?" Jericho says. "Why wouldn't you tell her?"

Jericho's voice is starting to feel overwhelming. He's not exactly screaming, but he might as well be.

"I didn't know what to do. I wasn't even sure if I saw what I saw till I confronted Dad a few days later."

"You actually asked him about it?" Lindsay asks.

"Oh, I didn't ask. I told him what I saw. Mom was at a yoga class and it was just me and Dad in the living room. He was on his laptop and I walked straight up to him and told him I saw who he was with in Niagara Falls."

"And what did he say?" I ask.

"Nothing at first. He just looked at me and I know he was probably wondering how he could lie his way out of it. But I was the same person at twelve that I am right now and Dad knew he couldn't bullshit me."

"So he admitted he was cheating?" Jericho sounds like he really doesn't want to hear the answer.

"That's not all he admitted. He told me he has another child."

I was waiting for everyone to gasp, but instead the room went still. The only real movement was James lifting his head in disbelief. I sat there and thought about what that meant. About how Ever felt when her dad straight up told her she has a half brother he's been keeping secret. Then I thought about Cy.

"What did Cy say when you told her?" I ask. Ever looks at me and shakes her head. "Oh ... Oh my God. She doesn't know?"

"I tried a million times to tell her. I recited it in my head over and over, but Dad made me promise. He told me it would crush my mom and that it didn't change anything in our family."

"And you believed him?" Jericho says.

"I don't know what I believed, but I never told Mom. And then Dad died and Mom got sick and I didn't know what to do."

Jericho gets up and tries to storm out of the basement. Ever tries to grab his hand, but he pulls away.

"You knew Dad had a whole other family and didn't tell Mom?"

"It's not that simple, Jericho."

"It's pretty simple to me."

Jericho keeps stomping and is up the stairs without another word. I want to chase after him and I probably should, but Ever just spilled her guts and she needs me to be here right now.

The rest of the BAGS still haven't said anything. I still haven't said anything. We all have our own drama. It's why we're here sitting around and forcing ourselves to talk about things we would otherwise never bring up. Ever's situation has so many layers, though, that it's tough to figure out where to even start. I shift even closer to Ever and loop my arm in hers.

"What your dad did is bullshit," Mark says. "Not just what he did, but the fact that he asked you to keep it a secret. It's bullshit."

"That's not the only time I saw them," Ever says. "They were at the funeral. The woman and her son. They were there when we buried Dad."

Trish and Chloe look at each other. Mark's still shaking his head. Lindsay hasn't moved since Ever started talking. I'm thinking of what to say. Something to make Ever know that I'm here for her. So many times, it's been the other way around. She's been so much like a big sister even though we're the same age. She's been the protector and now I need to step up.

"We need to find her," I say. "The only way you're gonna feel any kind of closure is if you talk to this woman face to face."

"No," Ever says. "I don't wanna do that."

"Candace is right," Lindsay says to Ever. "Knowing is better than not knowing. You don't wanna keep carrying this with you. Look what it's done to you already. It won't get any better."

"What about my mom?" Ever says. "Shouldn't we tell her first?"

"We'll tell her once we know everything," I say. "Right now all we know is what your dad told you. Let's get the full story and then we'll tell your mom."

"OK, but how are we gonna find her? The only thing Dad told me was her first name."

"Leave that to me," Lindsay says. "I have a Ph.D. in cyberstalking. If she's alive, I'll find her."

When everyone leaves, Ever and I take a bike ride down to the lake. It's not quite sundress weather yet, but we both feel just as comfortable in loose jeans and sweaters with no helmets to stop the wind from blowing our hair. The sun already starts to set by the time we're sitting next to each other on the rocks that rest on the edge of the lake. We're quiet for the first few minutes. You can see a straight line of the sun's reflection off the water. It's almost like this cosmic laneway that leads to only God knows where.

Ever's knees are to her chest and her arms are wrapped around her legs. It's still strange for me to think of her lying on that hospital bed. It's an image I haven't been able to make sense of yet. She's probably struggling with it too, but this is the first time we're actually going to have a full conversation since she asked me to leave her room.

"Do you think any of this shit is real?" Ever says. She's still looking out into the lake. "Like this whole world. How can it even be real? It doesn't even make any sense."

"I think it's as real as we want it to be. We're here, right. I see you, you see me. There's nothing fake about that."

Normally, we'd have a joint sparked by now, but when Ever came out of the hospital, we promised Cy no more drugs. That included weed. "At least for a couple of months," she said.

Ever fought it a little bit, but I agreed with Cy. Ever's mind should be clear. She didn't need anything affecting her decision making.

"I don't mean it's fake. I mean, like, everything is already as it's supposed to be. The lake, those ducks, the fish swimming in the water. They don't consider anything past their purpose. We're the only ones that make shit up. We made everything in this world up and gave it a purpose when we're really not in any position to give anything purpose since we don't even know why we're here."

I don't even know what to say when Ever gets like this, so I don't say anything.

"So," Ever says. "No more fake mom, eh?" She smiles and spins her body towards me. "How the heck did that happen?"

I recap every detail of the story up to our last phone call about my former fake mother possibly going on some kind of meds.

"Wow. You're like the last decent teenager left on the planet," Ever says. "I don't know if I could've forgiven her like that, much less taken her in and gotten her help. My pettiness would kick in at some point."

"You're way nicer than you think, Ever. But don't worry, I won't tell anyone."

I say it jokingly, but I know Ever's heart is bigger than she lets on. She just hates feeling things, or too many things I should say. She still expects things to be simple and when they're not, she finds her own way.

"So what now?" Ever asks. "You think you'll actually have some kind of relationship with her? Is that even what you want or you just want her to get better?"

"I'm not even sure yet. We talk. I'm not sure what's gonna come after that."

Ever's back to gazing over the lake. There's so much to think about that I'm surprised she's been this attentive. I want to ask her about her dad. About if she really wants to go through with finding this woman. But there's only shade now. Our shadows have disappeared and the water is calm. There's nothing to say.

## JERICHO

"IT'S PRETTY SIMPLE TO me," I say, then hustle up the stairs and away from the group. Mom's standing in the kitchen talking to the chef. Her elbows are leaned over the countertop and she's picking at something the chef's left on a plate. Ever has no idea what she's talking about. There's no way Dad would do something like that. Why would he? He loved Mom and he knew how much she loved him.

I can hear him telling the annoying story of how they met. I see his arms moving in the air as he's talking. Mom's rolling her eyes even though she told me she still gets butterflies thinking about how Dad came knocking on her door.

I should just tell her right now. Tell her everything Ever just said so we could laugh about it. I bet she'd say something to defend Ever's imagination, but remind me that Dad loved his family. He probably still loves us from wherever he is right now.

But why? Why would he do that? Let's say for one minute that this isn't some kind of bad dream and Ever's telling the truth. How could Dad just randomly have another family running around without Mom knowing? I get that he travels a lot, but so does Candace's dad and he's not out there with his own harem. Our family was happy. We didn't grow up having to close our bedroom doors to block the noise from our parents arguing. We didn't wake up to see Dad sleeping on the couch or ever hear Mom threaten to leave. I can count on one hand how many times I even heard either of them raise their voice at each other.

I should tell Mom right now. Walk right up to her and tell her everything. Her hand's under her chin. Her smile is Ever. The way she chews the food a million times before swallowing is Ever. It's like Ever took so much of Mom that there wasn't enough left for me to have any. I'm thinking all of this knowing that there's no way I'd ever tell Mom anything to hurt her. She's the strongest person I know but everyone has limits. Everyone has their breaking points.

"You guys finished already, Jericho?"

And that's the difference. In just a few words you can feel Mom's compassion. Her voice on its own can make moments better. Where Mom's like a blue jay nursing her eggs in a nest she built herself, Ever's more like a hawk ready to swoop down and kill its prey.

"No, I just need to grab something from my room." I don't even know how long I've been standing here thinking of what to do. Once I'm in my room, not even Kendrick Lamar can save me. I'm taking it all the way back to "Section .80" and my thoughts still won't stop. Ever's not lying. I know that. But there's more to the story and I'm just as sure of that too. The only reasonable thing to do is find that woman. She'll let us know everything and maybe then we can tell Mom. Because one way or another, Mom needs to know.

When I text Candace my thoughts, she says the BAGS feel the same way. Apparently, Lindsay works for Anonymous or something and says she can find her.

"She says give her a couple of days," Candace texts back. Which is great because I need a break from this shit. Between Candace's fake mom coming back and Ever telling me I might have a half-brother somewhere out there, the only thing I can think about is inhaling some weed smoke. And James is still downstairs so I won't have to do this alone. I wait till I hear the front door open and close a few times before heading back down. I already texted James to let him know and he's waiting outside when I get there.

"I don't think it's a good idea," James says. We end up in his backyard. No one's at his house, so we're smoking under the pergola and drinking Heineken out the bottle. "We shouldn't be going after this lady."

I'm actually a bit surprised because James usually likes a good adventure.

"If she was at the funeral like Ever said she was," James says. "then that means she knows your dad had a family. She obviously didn't care to mix with your family when your dad was alive, why would she want to talk to any of you now?"

"That all makes sense," I say. "But I don't think you get it. This isn't a logical situation for us. We don't know shit about this lady and her kid except what my dad told Ever years ago. I think we at least need to get some answers."

James just keeps puffing. He doesn't say anything and I know he still doesn't agree with me. I'm pretty sure he also knows that no matter what he says, we're finding this lady.

"Anyways, I'm headed back home."

"I'm gonna come with you," James says. It's kind of strange he wants to come back with me since his stepmom isn't here, but he's been a bit off since Ever went to the hospital so I'm not thinking much of it.

When we get inside, I head straight for my bathroom and I hear James say hi to my mom. This is a number two type situation so I'm in here for at least five minutes. Right before I'm done, I hear Ever and Candace coming back inside. When I get out, my mom's standing in front of the bathroom door with James a bit behind her, avoiding my eyes.

"Motherfucker."

## CANDACE

CY'S SITTING ON THE loveseat on her own. Ever and I are on one couch and Jericho's sitting on the floor with his arms folded. He and James really got into it a little while ago. I didn't even realize Jericho could get that upset till I heard the stuff that was flying out of his mouth. He got right up in James' face when he realized he told Cy everything. Ever had to jump in the middle and tell James to leave while I grabbed Jericho and walked him into the living room.

That's where we are now. I'd say things are a lot calmer, but that would be a lie. I can't tell if this is tension or anticipation, but either way, it's heavy enough to feel. We all want to know what Cy has to say about this. She's taken her time making herself a cup of tea. The steam's still floating just above the cup, but Cy keeps it in her hand.

"Ever, I'm sorry your father made you keep that secret. It must've been so hard for you not to say anything for so many years."

"Hard went away, like, the first year," Ever says. "It's been impossible. And I'm sorry you had to find out like this, Mom. That's not how we planned it."

Cy has a light smile on her face.

"I've heard about your plan. And I get it. You all want to help and thought you were doing me a favor by not telling me, but I'm happy you didn't go looking for Reyna."

Jericho unfolds his arms.

"Wait," he says. "How do you know her name?"

Cy takes a deep breath and puts her tea on the coffee table.

"That's what we need to talk about. I knew about your father and Reyna. It wasn't a secret. I knew from the very beginning."

Whatever traces of anticipation were left have been overtaken by the looks on Ever and Jericho's faces.

"Mom," Ever says, "what are you saying? You knew the whole time that Dad was having an affair?"

"No, I'm saying that it wasn't an affair."

"So what was it?" Ever asks.

Cy glances at each of us. She's thinking about how much she should tell us. About how detailed she should get or how much truth is too much truth. But she knows where Ever was just a couple weeks ago. She knows how sensitive Jericho is about his father. She takes another deep breath.

"You know what, I can't." Cy stands up. "I can't do this right now. I know you kids want answers, but I just can't right now. I'm sorry."

Cy walks out of the living room and up the stairs. It's funny how tension and confusion can feel the same.

"What just happened?" Ever asks. Jericho and I don't say anything. What could we say? We all saw the same thing, which none of us have seen before. Cy doesn't run away from anything. Ever.

"I don't get it," I say.

Jericho's still sitting on the floor. None of us know what to do.

"I get it," Jericho says. "We need to find Reyna."

# CANDACE

IT TOOK A FEW weeks, but I'm starting to understand what Ever meant when we were sitting by the lake. Some things just don't feel real. It's like we're all in a movie without a script, just making shit up as we go. That's definitely how I feel today. Just a couple of months ago, I would've never imagined speaking to my former fake mother again. And even if that image somehow entered my mind, there was no script for me welcoming her back into my life. But here we are.

I've been staring at myself in the mirror for at least five minutes. I've changed three times already and now I'm thinking that this skirt is a bit too short, but Julia's going to be here any minute so it'll have to do. I really shouldn't even care this much. It's not like we haven't been talking almost daily for the past two months. Most of it recently has been through text, but I should be comfortable enough not to still be playing with my hair.

I've learned so much about her since she showed up outside our house. She's a personal support worker, which got me kind of angry when she first told me. It's like she can only take care of other people when she gets paid, but taking care of her child was impossible. But she explained that she only got that job a few years ago. Before that, when she first had me, she usually worked in customer service or some kind of hospital admin jobs.

She doesn't have any other kids and doesn't know who my father is. At least that's what she says and I really don't care so I don't press her on it. She stopped talking to her sisters a long time ago. She said last time she spoke to them, they were both in Jamaica. She's not sure if they're still there.

Every new piece of information is like a step. Small ones, but steps nonetheless. At first, I was more guarded about sharing stuff about my life. That bitterness hadn't left my soul yet and revealing bits of myself to a woman who abandoned me wasn't something I was ready for. Not right away. Then when I finally did start opening up, I felt guilty. Retelling stories of private jet flights with my dad and month-long stays at ranches in Florida or even our nanny made me feel bad. Not because I had never recognized my privilege, but retelling it felt like showing off even though it was my real life.

"You look great, sis." Ever's sitting on the edge of my bed. No way she's missing this. The fact that we weren't talking the first time Julia popped back up was all the reason she needed. Plus, if Julia was going to be part of my life, she'd have to get to know the biggest part of it. "I'd hate to be here when you're getting ready to see my brother."

Nanny has dinner ready to go just as we're all getting seated. We're at the dining room table, which is odd for us. We're used to eating around the island in the kitchen or on the couch in the living room or even in the basement. The dining room is usually for when Dad has one of his coworkers over and we do the formal thing. But it works for today too. The table's long enough to fill a middle school classroom, but Mom set up the seats so that we're all sitting in the middle. Mom and Dad are on one side and I'm sitting in between Ever and Julia on the other.

"You really do have a beautiful home," Julia says. "It gets more magnificent every time I'm here."

I guess she has been here twice before even though this feels like the first time she's been welcome.

"Thank you, Julia," Mom says. "We've been here a long time now so we've made a lot of changes over the years, but this is home."

Julia's in a black blouse and a long, slim-fitting skirt. Mom is far more casual, as usual, although the gray pantsuit she's wearing does have some flare to it. Dad's in a white dress shirt with blue jeans which may as well be his uniform and Ever's in an emerald green dress with a thin diamond necklace. Glasses of red wine are already poured and standing beside plates of a Jamaican dish only Nanny could cook up.

"I'd like to say a few words," Mom says. Everyone lifts their glasses and adjusts the napkins on our legs. "I would be lying if I said I saw this day coming, and I'd be an even bigger liar if I said it didn't scare the hell out of me. But Candace has opened her heart and the least we can do is open our home. Cheers to new beginnings."

We all air tap our glasses and start passing around plates.

"Thank you," Julia says. "For everything. It does feel good being close to Candace again and her family. Although I haven't had the pleasure of meeting you yet, Ever. Candace tells me you two are sisters."

I've told Julia endless stories about Ever. She pretty much knows everything from the day we met. I left out the recent stuff, though, so she doesn't know about the hospital or anything about Ever's mom.

"We are sisters," Ever says. "Been sisters since we were five years old."

"That's a beautiful thing," Julia says. "I wish I had that kind of bond with my real sisters, but they all hate me."

"Candace is my real sister," Ever says abruptly.

"Of course she is. I didn't mean it like that. I know how close you two are to each other and I think it's special."

Everyone's plates are clean when Nanny clears the table. Glasses are refilled for the third time before Nanny comes back out holding an orange-colored cake with white icing and some kind of gold decorations on the top. I'm hoping it's what I think it is.

"Dessert for everyone," Nanny says. "I don't want to hear that you all are full."

We know better than to refuse any of Nanny's treats. And when she cuts into it and I see that it's carrot cake, which she knows is my absolute favorite, I get my spoon ready even though I barely have any room left in my stomach. Ever has her spoon in hand too. She's had this carrot cake almost as many times as I have.

"This looks wonderful," Julia says. "Do you all eat like this every day?"

"What do you mean?" Mom asks.

"I just mean that there are so many different dishes and all of them were delicious. I couldn't imagine eating this good every day."

I could tell that Mom really didn't know what to say, so I jumped in.

"Nanny is the best. She's a part of our family and enjoys everything she does. We couldn't imagine life without her."

Ever's halfway through her carrot cake already and puts her spoon down.

"So Julia," Ever says. "I'm curious. What made you want to come back into Candace's life?"

I was ready for this. Actually, I'm surprised Ever waited this long to say something. But she was so tame during dinner that I knew it was only a matter of time.

"She's my daughter," Julia says. "I just wanted to be part of her life again."

"And what do you think made you leave in the first place?"

"Ever, sweetie," Mom says. "Let's not make Julia relive the past. She's here now and I think that's what's important."

"No, no," Julia says. "It's OK. It's something I have to live with every day of my life so it's fine. And to answer your question, Ever, I really wasn't in a good place. I was overwhelmed and when someone like me gets overwhelmed, it feels impossible to cope."

"And you think you're better now?"

"It doesn't exactly work like that. I have good days and I have bad days. The difference today is that the bad days don't push me over the edge."

Ever seems satisfied with those answers. My dad is loving every minute of this. For someone who's so professional, he gets excited by a little drama.

"And how are those sessions working out for you," Dad asks. "You obviously seem to be much more, umm, calm." My mom looks at Ever, Ever looks at me, I look at Julia and we all start laughing. "What? What did I say?"

"Thank you, sir," Julia says. "I do feel calmer. And thank you all for everything. Seriously. I can tell you've done such a wonderful job raising Candace considering ..."

"Considering what?" Mom asks, still coming down from her laughter.

"I mean, well considering that she's a Black girl and you two aren't Black."

"Why would that matter?" Ever asks. "They're her parents. That's never been a problem."

"That's always a problem, dear," Julia says. "You can pass so maybe your life has been different, but when you look at Candace, there's no mistaking who and what she is. It's not the same experience."

"And how would you know that?" Ever snaps. "How would you know what Candace's life was like when you just got here, like, yesterday? And just because I can pass doesn't mean anything. I'm Black just like you."

"Except you're not like me," Julia says. "And I know what Candace's life was like because I know what it's like being a Black girl. I can only imagine what she had to go through in this kind of environment."

It's the first time the table's been quiet all evening. Dad sits back in his chair while Mom sits up in hers and pulls it closer to the table. Ever looks like she's ready to jump over me and grab Julia by the hair.

"What do you mean this kind of environment?" Mom asks.

"I don't mean it in a negative way. You've obviously done very well for yourselves and given Candace everything we could never even dream of. But I'm sure there aren't a lot of girls who look like Candace in this world of yours."

"Julia," I say, "stop." I know what she means. I know what she's trying to say, but I also know how Mom and Dad are taking it and I don't want them feeling any kind of way because of Julia. "It's hard for Black girls in any world and this one isn't any different. But Mom and Dad have been with me through everything. They understand everything I've gone through."

Julia shakes her head and purses her lips.

"Mom and Dad understand?" she says sarcastically. "They can't understand, Candace. They can support you, but they'll never know what it feels like. And can we work on you calling me Mom? I know they're your family now, but I'm still your mother and it would be great if you could address me in the right way."

I can't believe what I'm hearing. Did those words just really come out of her mouth?

"Are you serious," Ever says. "You want her to call you Mommy? After, like, thirteen years of you being MIA you're all of a sudden a parent again?"

I turn to Ever and raise my hand to let her know she needs to chill out.

"Kinda funny how you want me to call you Mom now," I say. "But when I was, like, three or four years old you told me to call you Julia. Do you remember that? Because I do. I remember a lot. And this is my mom now so I call her Mom. And that's my dad so I call him Dad. There's no one else in this world or any world that deserves those titles more than they do."

Julia looks like she has a lot more to say, but she takes one look around the table and stands up. She opens her mouth to say something, but instead turns and walks to the front door. Her steps haven't changed. I don't even need to close my eyes to be back in my room at five years old hearing her pace back and forth on our creaky living room floor. It's a much longer walk to this front door, though, and I watch her the entire time. She doesn't look back when she walks out.

# JERICHO

EVER'S BEEN AT CANDACE'S house all day. I only know because I heard them talking on FaceTime last night about Candace's fake mom coming over. I guess that's been working out for her. I wouldn't know. Last time I spoke to Candace was over a month ago. Other than the times she's here, obviously, and even then it's just a wave or a hi-and-bye type of thing.

It's all my fault, of course. I ignored her texts and calls for a week after Mom dropped that bombshell on us. Or maybe I should say dropped half a bombshell because there's a lot more to the story. We all know that. I'm just the only one willing to do something about it. Ever's been acting like nothing's happened, which I don't get because she's the one who had to carry a secret for years that wasn't even a secret. She should be pissed. But she's not. I still hear her and Mom laughing in the backyard in the evening. They still sit shoulder to shoulder on the couch watching Chapelle reruns. Nothing's changed for them.

Nothing.

But I can't let it go. James thinks I'm overreacting. We still text once in a while, but I haven't seen him in a while either. He's never said sorry for telling my mom everything. In his mind, he hasn't done anything wrong, but he doesn't see what I see. From the outside looking in, what he did must feel noble or whatever. Like he did the courageous thing. But telling Mom before we knew the full story only made James feel better. My family's in no better position. At least, I wasn't. I don't know what the heck Ever's going through.

And I don't really care. How can they take the fact that we might have a brother out there so lightly? If it's true, Dad, our Dad, had another family. Did he read to his other son at night too? Do they have a chef and a four-bedroom house with another guesthouse and a backyard that flows into the trails and a cottage and a jacuzzi? What's this boy's name? Maybe Ever's willing to sit on these questions, but I'm not. Not at all.

We had a BAGS meeting. After everything went down with my mom and James, we still all met up. Ever made it happen. She said we needed to keep it going because even though it felt like these meetings stirred up trouble, that was the whole point.

"This is what it's supposed to feel like," she said. "All these emotions we're feeling were gonna come out sometime. It's a good thing that it's coming out now and coming out in this group. It's like you can't clean stuff up if you don't make a mess first. And at least part of all our lives is messy."

So we did it. We all gathered in my basement the same way we had before. This time we let Chloe tell her story. She told us about coming out to her family and how her dad took it well, but her mom just couldn't deal with it.

"She barely talks to me now," Chloe said. "We walk past each other at home. We don't go to the market on Sundays anymore. It's like she thinks I'm a different person just because I like girls."

Trish was right beside her the whole time and had a similar story. Candace was quiet and doing her best not to look at me, so was James. Luckily, whatever was going on between us didn't really change the atmosphere. It was as heavy as all of our other sessions and when it was over, Ever said she'd let everyone know when the next one was. She never did, but we still send messages in our group chat. Memes, mostly, although once in a while Ever or Candace will share some story about a teenager who committed suicide for reasons no one can figure out, or links to different articles or support-type groups that talk about a lot of the stuff we do in our sessions.

But it's not the same as meeting in person. And to be honest, I miss it. Even though Ever invited me as an afterthought, it felt good to be part of something. That's probably what everyone else felt too. None of us were on any sports teams. We all do extracurricular stuff with our families, but not at school. This group is our thing.

I'm over all of this reminiscing, though. I reached out to Lindsay to see if she would help me find Reyna, but she said she felt weird about it since Ever asked her not to. That pretty much left me on my own, but I'm getting used to that. And even though Lindsay said she wouldn't help, she did give me one big clue she found, which was Reyna's last name. That made things a little easier, at least that's what I thought. Reyna Blandon sounds like a unique name, except I couldn't find anyone on social media that fit. Either they looked like they were the wrong age or didn't come close to the vague description that Ever gave.

That's until I went on LinkedIn and saw someone who, at first glance, could pass for Mom. She had the same shape of face, the same dimples in her cheek, and her smile was just as wide as Mom's, although, that's where you started seeing the difference. But this woman looked like she could be about the same age as Mom and her name was a match.

That just happened last week. I got an email address that I knew would work because LinkedIn is all about business, but I haven't emailed her yet. If she is the real Reyna, as soon as she sees my name in the email, she'll probably block me and never reply. And even with my fake email, I'd have to have a very good reason to be reaching out to her. And if I want her to see me, she'd want to know I was a real person and then I'd be stuck.

So I'm in my room, "good kid, m.A.A.d city" is on repeat. My eyes are closed with my headphones on and I'm lying flat on my back thinking of what I can do. But I already know what I need to do. I mean, I already know who I need to talk to, but I don't know how to go about it. Because Ever would know exactly what to do now. She'd have a plan to get Reyna to agree to see us. Even though I have no idea what that plan is or how it would work, I don't need to know. Ever does. I'm sure of it. But I need to convince her that this is important. She thought it was at one point. I need to make her see the light again.

The only person who could make her understand is Candace, and she doesn't want anything to do with me right now. As true as that probably is, she's my only hope of convincing Ever. She's the only one Ever's ever listened to other than Mom. So as much as I'm hating myself for doing this, I send Candace a text of a white flag emoji and cross my fingers.

# CANDACE

WHAT DID I REALLY expect? That she would come back into my life and be what? What has she ever been to me? She's been my fake mom since the day I was cut out of her womb and she's still that today. It's my fault for thinking she could be anything different.

That hasn't stopped me from calling her number three times a day, or pressing send on messages I'll probably regret one day but feel good as hell to get off my chest right now.

*I should've never let you back into my life.*

*What a waste of time. You'll never change.*

*Hope you took some pics because you'll never see me again.*

I'm only going off like this because my fake mother didn't call or message me for a week after she left our place. Even when I messaged her right after she left and told her not to feel bad. That I was sorry we piled up on her like that and that this is new for all of us and is going to take some time to work. She read and ignored all of those messages, then stopped reading my messages altogether.

Those text messages were like a line of cocaine; momentary satisfaction that only felt good if I kept doing it. So I stopped.

And when the texts stopped, the crying started. That only lasted a couple of days, though. Ever wasn't having any of that. We were in my basement watching *Dear White People* because I was tired of being in my bedroom when I last broke out crying.

"Nope. Don't even try it," Ever said. "You're not giving that lady any more tears. Fuck that and fuck her. She's not worth it."

I still cried like a newborn, but Ever wouldn't let up.

"Who are you crying for, Candace? Who are you really crying for? She was never part of your life. The only mom that ever meant anything is still here. She's always been here."

I knew Ever was right and eventually, her words started penetrating. The truth is my life is better without my fake mother in it. I knew that. Mom and Dad made sure of that from day one. Even now, Mom hasn't said anything about what my fake mother did. She lets me vent, hugs me when she can tell I'm getting emotional and keeps the house running like normal. Like nothing's changed. And to be honest, nothing really has. I'm in the kitchen right now and Nanny's making sweet bread. Mom's in the living room reading a book and Dad's in Florida, where we'll all be soon enough. I'm in the living room too, on the couch beside Mom choosing classes for university. I decided to go to UBC, which Mom loved and hated when I told her. The thought of me being in university was enough, but soon I'd be on the other side of the country. She already had two flights booked.

"It's not too late to change your mind," Mom says, peeking at me from the corner of her eye. "You still have that offer from U of T."

Mom already knew my answer to this. She knew I wanted a true university experience, and that meant living on a campus where I wouldn't be able to just come home whenever I felt like it. Even though flying back and forth from BC is probably the same as other people taking a cab, I knew being that far away from home would change a lot for me. I needed my own space. UBC gave me that, plus they had the fashion business courses I really wanted to take.

I'm still browsing through courses when my phone buzzes again. Ever just left so I know it's not her, and when I see Jericho's pic I turn my phone around and leave it on the couch. It buzzes again though, and as much as I'm not feeling him right now, I still want to be there if he actually needs me.

The white flag emoji makes me laugh. The prayer hands are a bit too much, but I message back anyways.

"White flags are racist," I text back with about four laughing emojis.

"Come over," he replies. I ask him why and all he says is that it's important.

"OK. But it better be important for real."

Ever's not there when I get to Jericho's and he rushes me up to his room.

"I need your help," he says.

"Good to see you too, Jericho. Oh, you're sorry for being an ass-hole for the last few months? No problem. You're forgiven." He hates when I get this sarcastic. Says I remind him of Ever.

"Sorry, I'll apologize after we get through this. Right now, I need you to talk to Ever."

"About what?" We haven't even sat down. We're standing just inside his bedroom door that he closed as soon as we walked in.

"I found Reyna. At least I think I have. I saw her profile on LinkedIn." That's when we finally moved to his desk and Jericho showed me the picture of who he thought was Reyna.

"Wow, she looks just like ..."

"I know. It's strange, right? It's like Dad had a type or something."

"He definitely did." I can't tell if Jericho is scared or excited, "Did you message her?" Jericho tells me that he has her email address but hasn't messaged her yet. "Why not. You've obviously been at this for a while. Why not find out for sure?"

"That's why I need Ever. If this is Dad's mistress, I can't just invite her over. She's not gonna want anything to do with us. We need a plan to make this happen and I know Ever can figure it out."

I'm still looking at the picture, shocked at how much she looks like Cy. As much as I want to tell Jericho that I don't want to be involved, I know this means a lot to him. And when my fake mom first came around, he was there while Ever and I were going through our little not talking phase.

"So you want me to convince Ever to make this happen?"

"Convince me to make what happen?" I swear Ever's a ghost. Neither of us heard the room door open, yet here is Ever standing right behind us like a Samurai Ninja. "And what are you guys looking at?"

I wonder if this is what it feels like to be caught cheating on your husband in your own house? I don't know what to say or what lie to make up. In some strange way, I guess this was the best possible outcome. Now we can get it over with right away.

"Look for yourself," Jericho says and we both move out of the way so Ever can see what's on the laptop.

"Is that ... how did you guys find her?"

"Jericho found her," I say. "I'm just finding out about all of this right now."

Ever's staring at the screen with her eyes squinted.

"Wow," Ever says. "She looks just like ..."

"Yeah, we noticed that too," I say.

Ever puts down the laptop and starts pacing around the room.

"I don't want to do this. I told you I'm over it, Jericho. Why would you dig her up?"

"Because you might be over it, but I'm not. Dad has a whole other family out there and we're acting like it's just another day in Oakville." Ever finally sits on the desk chair. "We need you, Ever. You gotta help us find a way to see her."

Jericho's phone's been buzzing the whole time. Guess he's been busy since he hasn't had any time for me. When it buzzes again I grab it to see the name, but just see a number.

"She must be new," I say and toss him the phone.

"It's not another girl, Candace. It's James's house phone, which is weird. Hold on." Jericho answers and puts the phone to his ear. He listens, turns away from us and walks to his window. "I'll be right there," He turns to us and says he has to go.

"What's going on?" I ask. "We're kinda in the middle of something."

"I know. It can wait. James locked himself in the bathroom. That was his dad. He thinks he has one of the kitchen knives."

Jericho's out the door before I can ask more questions.

"I'm coming with you," I say.

"Me too," Ever says. We jump in her car and we're there before we have time to talk about what we're really going to do. Why would James lock himself in the bathroom? And with a knife? I mean, I know he's a bit goofy, but this feels like a lot.

James's dad is waiting at the front door. Jericho hustles inside and we're right behind him.

"He's still in there," his dad says. We walk past James's stepmom who's on the couch smoking a cigarette. She doesn't even look at us.

Jericho pounds lightly on the bathroom door.

"Hey, buddy. You taking a shroom shit or what?" There's no response for a few seconds.

"Go away, Jericho. You shouldn't even be here."

"I'm not going anywhere, James. You know that. Why don't you let me in so we can talk?" James doesn't say anything. Jericho pounds the door a bit harder this time. "James, buddy, just let me in, bro. We can talk about whatever you want to. Just don't ... don't do this."

"There's nothing to talk about, Jericho. I want you to leave. My dad shouldn't have called you over here."

Jericho's about to pound the door again when Ever taps him on the shoulder. She moves Jericho aside and knocks on the door like she's a delivery person.

"James, it's Ever. Can you hear me?" No answer. Ever looks back at us and then sits on the floor. "Your stepmom didn't even look at us when we got in here. She must be a real bitch." I look at Jericho who's looking at James's dad whose eyes just got wide as an owl. "You don't have to answer that. I know she is."

James's dad can't stay still. He's biting at his nails and turning around to look at his wife in the living room who still isn't paying us any attention.

"You know your dad's out here with us, right? He called Jericho because he's scared you're gonna do something you can't take back.

And I've been there. I wanted to disappear after my dad died. Then when my mom got sick, there were some days I sat in my room for hours staring out the window. I don't even wanna tell you the thoughts that were going through my head, but I'm pretty sure you already know. But those are just thoughts, James. And thoughts aren't always real. What's real is that your father is out here right now because he loves you. Jericho is out here right now because he loves you. There's nothing fake about that."

Ever's head is down like she's about to pray. James still hasn't said anything and I can't help but to start wondering how this is going to end. I'm going to go out on a limb here and guess that James is high. And people don't make the best decisions when they're on drugs, especially teenagers. You can feel the anxiety coming from James's dad. He's in a salmon-colored, collared golf shirt tucked into a pair of khakis. I can see sweat spots under his armpits and more sweat on his forehead. He's skin bald, but I can see a shadow of where his hair used to be. On a good day, he looks a little bit like Taye Diggs.

"But she's not here." James's voice sounds distant coming from inside the bathroom. "She's not here and she should be."

"I know she's not here, James," Ever says. "But that's not your fault. The people who care about you are all here. And I know that's hard to swallow, but parents do shit sometimes that we can't understand. But you can't get stuck on things you can't change. It'll make you go crazy, trust me."

The door handle turns and Ever stands up quickly. James opens the door, but doesn't step out. The knife is on the floor behind him. His eyes are red and glossy and it looks like he hasn't done his braids in weeks. Without a word, his dad bear hugs him and starts crying. James's head is in his dad's chest and he's crying too. James reaches his hand and pulls in Jericho.

James's stepmother isn't on the couch anymore when we walk past. His father is standing with us at the door telling Ever and Jericho thank you for the hundredth time.

"I knew you were the right person to call, Jericho. And thank God you came, Ever. I don't want to think what would've happened if you weren't here."

When we get to Ever's car, she puts both hands on the wheel, but doesn't turn on the ignition.

"I know how we can get Reyna to see us."

## CANDACE

JERICHO'S LAPTOP IS STILL open when we get back to the house. Ever slides into the chair while Jericho and I hover over her. The password screen pops up and before Jericho says anything, I reach over Ever's shoulder and type in *HotTubLove*. When Jericho pretends to be surprised, I wink and blow him a fake kiss.

"Look," Ever says. We're all staring at Reyna's LinkedIn page. "It says here that she's a family counsellor."

"So what?"

"So who needs more counselling than our family right now?"

"True, but she knows who you and Jericho are. You can't just call her and book an appointment. She'll ignore it."

"She's not talking about our family." For once, Jericho is keeping up with Ever more closely than I am. "Ever, you're a fucking genius."

Both of them are looking at me like a plate of their chef's seafood.

"No way," I say. "It's not happening."

"It's the only way, Candace," Jericho says. "We need a real situation to get into the room with Reyna. Your situation is more than real. We have to do this."

"We don't have to do anything. This is about you and Ever figuring out your situation. I already tried with my fake mother. I'm not going through that again."

"Candace." Ever sounds so much like her mother when she gets serious. "Both of you are wrong. When I said 'our family' I meant all of us. We're all family in here. And right now, the only way all of us can at least try to fix this is if you click on this link and book an appointment."

My arms are folded and I'm shaking my head. I don't want to do this. At least I don't think I do. How many times do I let my fake mom disappoint me before I get the point? The only thing keeping me from walking out of Jericho's room right now is that I still feel bad about how things ended with Julia. I feel like her walking out of dinner was my fault and that I should've gone after her. She really was trying, but maybe it was us who wasn't ready.

"She'll never do it," I say. "She's not returning any of my messages. She doesn't even read them anymore."

"Let me worry about that," Jericho says. "Just book that appointment?"

*This is stupid. It's never going to work.* Those thoughts are running through my mind at the same time I'm choosing a date for an initial consult with Dr. Reyna Blandon.

"It's gonna work, sis. Trust me."

It's so easy to believe everything Ever says, but this time I'm not sure. I don't even know if what we're doing is right. Because the situation with me and my fake mom is a real thing, and to use that as some kind of Trojan horse to confront Reyna about her history with Ever's mom and dad feels shady.

"There's something they're not telling us, Candace." Ever's

reading my mind again. "And I know this plan feels a little devious, but it really is the only way to get this weight off my chest. You saw what it could do to me. We both have a chance to fill some leaky holes in our lives. We should take it."

"And what about me," Jericho says. He's made his way to the bottom of his bed. "I don't have holes in my life?"

"You have craters, Jericho. It'll take more than family therapy to fix whatever you're going through."

Ever nudges me, flashes her sharpest smile and wraps her arms around my shoulders.

"You're the best, sis. You've been the best since I taught you how to spell your name."

Ever leaves Jericho's room and I snatch my phone to follow her out.

"Hey." He grabs my hand and ushers me back inside the door. "Why don't you stay for a bit?"

Jericho has that same look in his eyes he did when he was seven and wanted to play with my paintbrush. As annoyed as I still am with him, I let him guide me to the bench across from his bed.

"Looks like you were right," I say. "Ever figured it out."

"She did. I think we're all kinda figuring things out as we go." I can't help but touch his face.

"How are you gonna convince my fake mom to do this?"

"Same way I convinced everyone to join BAGS."

"And that is?"

Jericho lifts me up like he's carrying an injured player off the field and tosses me gently on his bed.

"Like I said, let me worry about that. All you have to do right now is close your eyes."

## JERICHO

THE NEXT FEW DAYS feel like being waterboarded. It's like knowing your favorite rapper is putting out an album at midnight on Thursday and you're just sitting at your computer refreshing the page waiting for it to drop. Except multiply that anxiety by a thousand because the stakes are so much higher. This is my real life. And not just mine, all of ours. Dad, Mom, Ever, and now Candace. Whatever happens will affect our lives in ways I can't even think of right now. Whatever Reyna says, something is going to change.

Maybe that's a good thing. At least for me. I remember when Dad took me for a drive to Kingston. I was only nine or ten years old, but I was up in the front seat listening to him talk business through his Bluetooth. None of it made any sense to me, of course, but I still smiled when Dad winked at me and said, "Now that's how you close a deal."

When we got to Kingston, we'd walk through one of Dad's offices and everyone would say hi. Even at ten years old I could see the respect they had for him. I could feel how confident my dad was with telling people what to do. It's like he had all the answers at the tip of his brain just waiting for someone to ask the right question so he could let it spill out.

I don't have half of his ambition. I'm still trying to figure out what the heck I'm going to do with my life. If Dad was here, he'd know. He'd help me through it. I wouldn't be this confused. Not with him around. He always knew what he wanted and would've made sure I knew what I wanted too.

That's why I need to know. I can't just move off of this like it's not the most important thing in my life right now. Dad was everything to me. Everything to us. Is that how his other family felt too? Are they even really his other family?

Tomorrow's the day Candace scheduled the free consultation with Reyna. The morning after she booked the appointment, I called her fake mom. When she answered and I told her who I was, she hung up the phone. But then I texted her *Candace needs you* and she called right back.

"What's the matter? Is my daughter OK?"

"That depends on you," I said. "Candace is going through something. She's been going through something her whole life. And she's at the point where she either fixes that thing or buries it so deep that she'll forget it even exists. Which one do you want her to do?"

That kept her on the phone, and when I told her about the counselling session she said she'd give it a try.

"Only if this is really what Candace wants."

"It is."

That was half the battle. The other half was convincing Reyna to make the trip to Oakville instead of holding the session at her office in Hamilton. It's only a twenty-minute drive so we could've gone there no problem, but we needed it to be at Candace's house so we could sneak Mom in. Trying to somehow convince Mom to go to Hamilton and then walking her into Reyna's office just wouldn't work.

That's where the BAGS came in. We were talking about all of this in the chat when Trish had an idea none of us thought about.

*Just tell Reyna the truth*

*Huh?*

*Trish, you're losing me*

*So tell her that this is all an elaborate plot?*

*No I mean tell her that she needs to see how Candace lives to really understand the problem. She needs to walk the three minutes from the driveway to the front door and see her nanny and walk thru the home to really feel why all of that was intimidating to Candace's fake mom*

*But she can just tell her all of that*

*It's not the same and besides does anyone else have any better ideas???*

Nobody did so Candace emailed Reyna what Trish suggested and it worked. It actually wasn't even a big deal because Reyna said she does house calls all the time, especially for initial consultations.

*Being in the home helps me get a better understanding of what I'm up against when we officially start therapy* is how Reyna responded.

The morning Reyna's supposed to come over to Candace's, we're already at her house for breakfast. It's only eight o'clock so I know none of us can sleep. I messaged Candace at 7:00 only to find out Ever was already over there and both of them were wide awake. Candace has a cup of chai ready for me by the time I get there. We're all sipping something sitting around the island in her kitchen, silently praying for the numbers on our phones to move faster. I finally say what I know we're all thinking.

"You think she'll actually show up?"

"Why wouldn't she?" Candace says. "This is her job. She'll be here."

"I meant your fake mom. You think she'll actually show?"

"Of course she will," Ever jumps in. "Everything is gonna work exactly like we said it would."

I'm not sure I've ever seen my sister nervous. She's talking like she's sure, but doesn't look me or Candace in the eye when she says it. I don't know, maybe I'm wrong. Maybe Ever is totally confident and I'm the one not sure about any of this.

We spend the rest of the morning and early part of the afternoon in front of the TV. Didn't really matter what was on. We just need to be distracted. Then Candace's doorbell rings and we all scramble to grab our phones.

"We said six o'clock, right?" Ever says. "There's no way she's here this early."

"No way," says Jericho as Candace walks to the door. She pauses for a second and I can see her closing her eyes and taking a deep breath. When she opens the door, Lindsay's blonde hair looks like it fills the doorway.

"We're here." Lindsay brushes past Candace, followed by Trish and Chloe, then Mark with his Raptors cap loosely on his head.

"Ummm." Candace is still standing at the door holding it open. "What are you all doing here?"

"What are we doing here?" Trish repeats.

"You didn't really think we'd let you guys go through all of this without us, did you?" That's Chloe right on cue. We look at Mark and he shrugs his shoulders.

"I just do as I'm told," he says.

I'm looking at Ever, who's looking at everyone and I'm not sure if she's flipping out or about to huddle everybody together for a group hug.

"So let me get this straight," Ever says. "All of you think you're gonna stay here while we go through this whole ... situation?"

Lindsay nods her head. Chloe and Trish lock arms and nod their heads too. Mark smiles and shrugs his shoulders again.

"I fucking love you guys," Ever says. We all break out laughing when a voice interrupts our moment.

"Isn't this a happy scene."

Candace's fake mom is standing just inside the doorway. She's holding a red purse with a leopard print shawl thrown over her shoulders.

"You didn't tell me this was group therapy, Jericho." We're all staring waiting for someone to say something. "I knew this was a bad idea."

Julia turns around and tries to leave.

"Wait." Candace grabs her elbow. "Just wait. This is not what it looks like. These are my friends. They're just here to support me, that's it. They're not sitting in the room with us. But they've all become an important part of my life and so I want them to stay. They deserve to stay."

Candace's nanny is at the top of the staircase watching all of this. Julia still looks like she wants to bolt out of here.

"You're already here. Let's just go downstairs and try to work this thing out."

I can tell she's still skeptical, but Julia unwraps her shawl and walks towards the basement. Candace follows her down and the rest of us spread out on the couches.

"I can't believe you're all here," Ever says. "If it wasn't for this group, I never would've talked about what I saw that day and never would've had the nerve to confront my mom about it."

"This was your idea," Lindsay says. "You made all of this happen. We just showed up."

Another ring of the doorbell steals our attention.

"OK," Ever says. "It's showtime."

## CANDACE

JULIA IS SITTING ON a floor pillow up against the wall in the basement. She hasn't let her eyes slip sideways once and her nails tapping against the floor tile sound like hail hitting the window. I'm sitting beside Julia, but not next to her. It's like we're two kids who've been sent to the principal's office for a schoolyard scrap. Reyna's sitting in front of us with her legs crossed and a recorder on her lap. All she needs is a pair of tights and she'd pass for a yoga instructor.

"This is a beautiful home, Candace. You mentioned in the intake form that you were adopted into this home when you were five years old. Is that right?"

"Yeah, my mom and dad brought me here when I was five. I wasn't officially adopted till I was almost seven."

"And I'm assuming your home is the one she left, Julia?"

"I left her." Julia hasn't smiled or frowned since she walked through the front door. "I left her alone for twelve years."

"You left me by myself for two days," I say. "I haven't felt alone since my mom found me in my room."

I know the BAGS are at the top of the staircase trying to listen to every word, even though they probably can't hear much with the door closed. Ever will be leaving to get her mom soon. My guess is the boys and girls won't be the only ones screaming today.

Reyna nods her head at my last statement.

"This is not your first time in this house. Is that right Julia?"

"You already know that's right. The only reason we're here is because I walked out of this house."

"I don't want to make any assumptions, Julia. I want to make sure I'm getting all the facts straight before we move forward."

"Facts? You want facts? Let me help you out. My daughter doesn't like me. And she has very good reasons not to. I left her alone at five then came back a few months ago throwing rocks at that front window right upstairs. Instead of her new family calling the cops, they put me in therapy. That worked for a while until they ran me out of this house last time I was here. So yeah, you want facts? Those are it."

Reyna looks at me like she wants me to confirm what Julia just said.

"Everything is true except no one ran you out of here, Julia." Her eyes catch mine for the first time since we've been in the basement.

"Oh really? So what would you call it when four people gang up on one person? Should I have just sat there and taken that?"

"Slow down, Julia," Reyna says. This must be so normal for her because she doesn't seem bothered at all by the tension that's crept into this room. "You said four people ganged up on you. That would be Candace and her parents. Is there someone I'm missing?"

"Yes. Candace's best friend. She started the whole thing, that one. Says her and Candace are sisters. Her name is Ever, I think."

"Ever?" Reyna's mouth drops. She looks at me and I can see her thoughts like we're in the movie Inside Out. "Ever is your best friend?"

I lean back against the wall and don't say anything. I'm thinking about the BAGS at the top of the staircase and praying one of them busts in here and saves me. Is Ever even back yet? Is Cy with her?

Reyna throws her recorder in her purse.

"I have to go," she says. Julia looks confused.

"Reyna, wait," I say. "Please, just wait."

"Did you know?" she says. "Is that what this is all about? Did you know?"

Reyna speeds up the staircase and I'm hustling to keep up. The BAGS are at the top of the door when she bursts through. No Ever in sight though, which means this whole plan is about to implode.

"Reyna," I say again. "Reyna, please. Just give us a minute to explain everything." She's already at the door.

"Sorry, Candace. I can't be part of whatever this is. I need to go. Right now. I hope you and your birth mother find the help you need."

Reyna pulls the door open and Ever is standing in the doorway with Cy right beside her.

## CANDACE

THIS IS MESSY. SO messy. Reyna and Cy are staring at each other, but neither of them have said a word. Ever's looking at me with her WTF face and I'm shaking my head because we were all so stupid to think this would work.

"Reyna?" Cy finally breaks the awkwardness. "What are you doing here?"

Julia has made her way upstairs. She's standing behind the BAGS, but looks just as clueless as Cy. I can't help but think that part of her is enjoying this chaos. She must be taking some pleasure in seeing cracks in my "perfect" world.

"I have a feeling Candace and Ever can answer that."

"Ever?" Cy looks at Ever then at me. "Girls, what's going on here?"

"OK," Ever starts, "let's just all go inside. Reyna, I know you're probably losing it right now, but you're already here. At least let us explain. If you wanna leave after that, it's up to you."

Staying is the last thing Reyna wants to do, but Ever has that stubborn look on her face and even though they don't know each other, I'm sure Reyna can tell that there's only one right move.

"And what about them?" Reyna asks and points at the BAGS. "Are they staying, also?"

"They're half the reason we're even here," Ever says. "We're gonna tell them everything, anyways, so they might as well hear it all now."

Reyna shakes her head and gives a little chuckle.

"Back downstairs we go, then."

We all move downstairs like a small procession heading to Sunday service. Even though we're at my house, the BAGS sit in the same order they would if we were at Ever's. Cy and Reyna fill out the semicircle while Ever hasn't sat down yet. We're all staring at her while she stands like a boxing referee about to explain the rules of the match.

"Mom, I know this is weird, but we had to do it. It's the only way we could get you to tell us the truth. The fact that you know each other already proves that there's so much more to the story than you're telling us."

"You didn't have to do anything, Ever. You chose to do this." Cy's tone is sharper than I'm accustomed to. "I told you to leave it alone. Both of you." Cy flashes some daggers at Jericho who looks away.

"Let me just ask one question," Reyna jumps in. "Candace, do you and your mom actually have problems or was this entire thing a setup?"

I totally forgot about Julia. She's not in the basement and when I run upstairs calling her name like three-year-old me begging for some attention, her shawl is gone. Ever's right behind me as I'm staring at the front door.

"It's OK, sis," Ever says. "I know we keep thinking about how hard this is for you, but it's probably a lot for her to handle too. Give her some time. You have more than enough love in this house."

I'm not surprised. I'm not sad. Maybe I'm a little bit angry and disappointed, but Ever's right, there's a lot of love in this house. Even though my mom's not here and my dad's still in Florida, it's like they've transported the energy that's keeping me strong right now.

"OK, sis, time to go deal with my family drama. You ready?"

Ever holds out her hand and I take it. We walk hand in hand back to the basement.

"No questions, please," I say. "We can deal with all my stuff later. Let's get back to the people who are actually here."

Ever and I take our place on the floor. We're still holding hands and I can feel hers start to shake.

"Like I was saying," Ever says. "I know this is a lot, Reyna, but think about what Jericho and I are going through right now. We have no idea what's going on and you can change that. I saw you with my dad in Niagara Falls. I know you guys had something. Why don't you just tell us what's happening?"

"Stop," Cy interrupts. "We can't be doing this. You don't even know what you saw, Ever. None of you understand what's happening here."

"So tell us, Mom." Jericho is sitting diagonally from Cy. "Make us understand. You always say there's nothing we can't get through, so let's get through this."

Cy shakes her head and looks over at Reyna who's sitting cross legged with her purse in her lap.

"We said if it came to this, we'd tell them," Reyna says. Cy still looks defiant. She's scanning the room and I can tell she's thinking of a way to make this all go away. Even with her stroke, Cy can still sit with both legs tucked under her bum like she's about to start one of her daily yoga sessions.

"You kids," she says. "And you're sure you're OK with everyone hearing this?" She directs that question to Ever and Jericho.

"This group has helped us get this far," Ever says. "They might as well be here for the end of it."

Cy takes a deep breath.

"Wait," Ever says. She takes the silver ball out of her pant pocket and rolls it over to Cy. "Now you're ready."

Cy cups the ball in both hands and starts her story.

"Your father has to be the most persistent man I know. Not a lot of men can handle the kind of rejection I put him through. He wanted to get married so badly and I just didn't. And I know part of it was the kind of lifestyle I lived back then. I didn't ever think I would be with one person forever."

I see Mark's eyebrows get narrow. He doesn't know Cy so he must be wondering what kind of lifestyle she's talking about.

"But there was another reason marriage was something I wanted to avoid. And ..." Cy looks at Reyna.

"It's OK," Reyna says. "They love you." Cy's eyes are getting teary, but she keeps going.

"The thing is," Cy says, "I can't have kids. I've known that since I was in my early twenties." Now it's Ever and Jericho's turn to look at each other. "And I knew how important it was to your father to be a parent. It's all he ever talked about. So when I told him having kids wouldn't be possible, I thought that would be the end of it. But he stuck with me. He kept coming back and told me he loves me more than anything in this world and that we'd figure it out."

Now Reyna's eyes are tearing up.

"And after we got married, I met Reyna. And we became friends. We looked so similar that people thought we were sisters. And I told her everything about your father and I and she wanted to help, so she offered to be a surrogate. I knew right then that the universe put her in my life for a reason."

The first tear slips down Ever's face. Jericho hasn't changed expressions. The room is as silent as a closed closet.

"It didn't take any convincing to get your father on board. He was so excited when I told him I wanted to do it. And so we did it. Reyna became our surrogate for both of you, one year after the other. But we knew what it meant for our friendship. We didn't want you kids to grow up thinking you were any less of my children than you are so we agreed we'd keep our distance."

"I only had one condition," Reyna says. "I wanted a child of my own. One that kept Cynthia and I connected forever. Cynthia and your father thought about it and years after you two were born, your father gave me my own child."

"And that's who you saw, Ever," Cy says. "Your father would spend time with Reyna and her son even though her son had no idea who your father really was."

I'm trying my best not to let my face show everything that's running through my mind. I have so many questions. So many things I want to know. Like how didn't anybody know about this. How were they able to keep this a secret for so long?

"Why?" Ever can barely get her words out. "Why wouldn't you just tell us? Why keep it a secret for so long?"

"We wanted to tell you, sweetheart. We did. But then things started to change. Your father's business started doing really well and he did all of it on his own. He never took a dime from my parents. So he wanted to move away from the city. He said we could start another life for ourselves out here. Somewhere no one really knew who we were or about anything else. Then years passed by and after a while, it just didn't make sense to tell you kids."

"So you didn't think it was important to let us know you're not our birth mother?" I can't imagine what's going through Cy's head right now. Ever is hers. That's all she knows. Until this moment, that's all Ever knew. Where does Cy even go from here?

"I'm your mother. That's what I thought was important. It's the only thing that mattered."

Jericho gets up and slowly starts walking away from the group and up the stairs. Cy doesn't say anything to stop him. Ever doesn't look like she has the strength to move. Her face is damp and she doesn't bother wiping it.

"This doesn't make any sense," Ever says. "How ... I mean, how didn't we know? I don't get it."

"I know it's a lot," Cy says. "I can't imagine what you're thinking. But this doesn't change anything, Ever. You're my daughter and I love you and your brother more than anything."

I want to say something. I've been here. Everything that Ever's feeling right now I've felt a million times over. Even though it's not the exact same situation, I know the confusion that's tearing her apart. It's something she'll have to learn how to live with for the rest of her life.

"BAGS, why don't you all wait upstairs," I say. "We'll be up in a bit."

No one says anything. They exit single file out of the basement, each of them tapping Ever on the shoulder when they walk past her. Cy, Ever, Reyna, and I are still sitting in our same spots. Ever's staring into the floor. Cy and Reyna are staring at Ever. It's the first time in my life when I genuinely feel that words won't make any sense. There's nothing that could be said to make any of this more manageable. I cuff my arm around Ever and let her head rest on my shoulder.

"I want you to know that I'm so blessed to be able to give Cy this gift," Reyna says. "You and Jericho are the most incredible parts of her life. She is your mother, Ever. I don't look at it any other way."

"Except the fact that you gave birth to me." That's not just sarcasm in Ever's voice. Her mind probably feels like it's about to explode and she's doing whatever she can to keep it together. "Which means you are my mother in a lot of ways."

"But not the most important," Reyna says. "Cy is the one who's been here with you, Ever. She raised you. Everything you are is because of her and your father."

"So I guess a big part of me is a liar." Ever pulls out of my arms and stands up. "I don't know how you expect me to be OK with this. None of this is OK. I don't even know what to think. I've been carrying this weight for years thinking that Dad had this secret life. And he did. You both did."

Cy and Reyna don't say anything. They watch Ever leave the basement and still have no words. I get up to leave too.

"Protect your mind," I say to neither of them in particular. "At all costs."

# EVER

BEING AWAY FROM CANDACE is way harder than I thought. We still Face-Time almost every day and text like we don't know anyone else, but it's not the same. I miss her reading one of her fashion books on my bed. I miss our backyard walks. We'd both get so high and spend the rest of the evening eating and talking about stuff we'd forget the next day. I miss her so much. And when I get a message at ten in the morning, which is like 7:00 a.m. BC time, I know she misses me too.

Candace says she'll be back for Christmas and I'm trying my best not to count down the days. It wasn't even possible to imagine my life without her just over a month ago. Then she left for university and it was like my heart split in half.

Mom would be proud of how dramatic that is. I guess everyone likes a little drama. I've had enough of it over the past year. Actually, ever since Dad died it's been one long episode of *This Is Us* and I'm over it.

So much would be different if Dad was still here. Mom would be different. Or I should say, Mom would be herself. She'd be that mother who let me sleep in her bed every time Dad was gone. That parent who would come out on the ice and skate with me when I was first learning. The Cy that Candace says is the coolest being God ever created.

I don't know what she is now. She's still my mother, I know that. Not my only mother. I wish I didn't know that. Those days of blissful ignorance are over, though. Now we're all trying to figure out what's next. Which pieces of ourselves that have just been shattered need to be mended. That's my goal in between Philosophy classes or evenings spent with new acquaintances at the library.

I live on campus even though I'm less than an hour away from home. It feels good to have my own space. Necessary, even. I still come home more than I should and let Chef remind me of what I'm missing. Mom loves it when I'm here. Even when I show up spontaneously it feels like she's been preparing. I'll walk right into a meal or just in time to catch the beginning of a *Jane the Virgin* episode. I've considered the possibility that Mom is tracking me and even asked her one day if she snuck that app on my phone. She denied it, of course, but I told her I'm not convinced. She laughed like it could be true.

True. Isn't that a funny word. I can say something right now that I believe with all my heart is real and that thing could be not true at all. It's like honesty and truth were separated at birth. Life would be much simpler if they were connected like the links on one of my chains, but that's not how they work. They're frenemies. *Mean Girls*. At the same time, both can be comforting when they're far enough apart. It's only when you put them side by side that they become explosive. Especially when they've been away from each other for a long time.

That's how I feel about this whole thing sometimes. That maybe I chased the truth a bit too hard and when I finally got it, it crushed my world. But maybe that wasn't such a bad thing. Maybe my world needed to be crushed. There are days I get so angry at myself for bringing Reyna and my mom together that I have to take a few deep breaths just to calm down. Other days, I know I did the right thing. I know that confrontation had to happen even though I had no idea where it would lead. Truth and honesty in the same room and I was the trigger they needed to explode.

This is when Candace would start looking at me all strange. Sometimes I go a little too deep. Then other times I talk more shit than a ball player. I catch her staring all the time. Most of the time I pretend not to notice and just let her think whatever she thinks. We've been sisters way too long for me to feel judged. Not by Candace. There's no one like her in this world.

I'm actually a bit jealous of her sometimes. How she's able to handle situations. Her fake mom left her when she still had baby teeth and she was ready to forgive her and take her back in. The only mother I ever knew tells me she didn't give birth to me, but raised me since I came out of Reyna's womb and I'm ready to cut all ties. Not really, but I don't have that thing that Candace has. I can't let things go as easily. I'm trying, but I can't find that part of me that can make any of this OK. Jericho can't either.

He's always been more sensitive. We're only one year apart, but it feels like he's my little, little brother. All the stuff I did to him growing up, it's amazing he hasn't pushed me off a balcony or something. He did start getting a bit tougher as he got older. I'll take some credit for that. But this Reyna thing hit him hard. He hasn't spoken to Mom at all since leaving the basement that day. Candace says she hasn't spoken to him since she's been away, but strangely enough, Jericho's been messaging me more than usual. Most of the time it's just him asking me about what I'm doing or what the parties in university are like. We haven't spoken about that day in a long time.

The only time we really spoke about it was the day after it happened. I went into Jericho's room the next morning and he was sitting up on his bed with his headphones on, of course. It looked like he hadn't slept at all. He was wearing the same clothes he had on the night before and the bags under his eyes looked like pebbles.

"Are you happy?" he asked me. "Do you feel better now that this is all out in the open?" Jericho's voice sounded raspy like he was just waking up.

"Why would I be happy about any of this?" I said. "It's not like I knew the truth. I thought Dad was having an affair or something. I didn't see all this coming."

"But don't you feel better? Isn't that the point of finding out the truth? Wasn't that what the whole BAGS thing was about? Getting all your feelings out so you can feel better about feeling messed up."

"The point of BAGS was for none of us to feel like we were alone."

"And how do you feel right now?"

I can't remember another time that Jericho ever made me feel like I was the little sister. He was looking straight at me, waiting for me to say something and I had nothing. No comeback. Nothing I could say that would've properly articulated what I was feeling. So I didn't say anything. Not at first. I walked up to his bed and sat down beside him. We stayed quiet for a few seconds before I could find any words at all.

"Are you gonna run away?" I asked him.

"What?"

"You should probably run away. You can't handle any of this so running away is your best bet right now. You can take my car. I won't report it stolen."

He must've thought that I lost my mind. He kept looking at me waiting for some kind of punchline, but I didn't say anything else. I got up and walked out of his room. That's pretty much how I've been dealing with this whole thing. Like it never happened. Like that day Mom and Reyna were honorary BAGS was some kind of twisted dream that I wish I couldn't remember.

The BAGS made it hard to forget though. They sent messages every day for weeks after it happened. It was all in good spirit and I know they just wanted to make sure Jericho and I were OK, but every vibration on my phone was like a trigger that put me back in Candace's basement. As many times as I typed "I'm good," I'm not sure I ever meant it.

We did have one more meeting before Candace left for school. It was more like a mini going away party, though. We started off in the circle, but instead of talking about our personal problems, we spoke about what we planned to do in the upcoming school year. Chloe and Trish were going to the twelfth grade. They were sad it would be their last year. Mark was happy his high school career was over. He's taking a year off before figuring out his next move.

James didn't come to our last meeting. He was about to start grade twelve too, but Jericho told me he'd been going to a real therapist. That's probably a good thing. I like to think that he wouldn't have gotten the help he needed if it wasn't for the BAGS.

We might not know how to solve all the problems, but we sure knew how to bring them to the surface. And isn't that the most important step? Or the hardest step? Just being able to recognize and say out loud that part of your life is fucked up, that's a big deal. Where would any of us be if we kept all that stuff inside?

Even though we missed James's energy at that last meeting, it was still a good time. We did it back at my house like usual. We actually tried to be somewhat responsible and didn't drink any alcohol or do any drugs. It was important we left the right memories. Who knew when we'd all be together again, and we'd all been to enough house parties by then to not have a craving to be drunk and high.

The thing I remember most about that evening was how much we laughed. We needed half a box of Kleenex for all of our other meetings, but there were no tears during that one. Even Jericho cracked a smile here and there.

"I'm gonna miss you guys." That was Candace right before we wrapped up for the night. She and I had already cried together a million times by then and when I heard her say that, I felt a little trickle trying to sneak out. "I didn't know what to expect when this group started, but I feel like we're all connected for life now."

And we are. All it takes is one of us to send a selfie of us at our desks or in our dorm rooms to kick off a round of conversations. It happens less frequently now, but it still happens. James even jumped in the last convo and the group went wild sending messages for hours.

It's such an escape from reality whenever I get into that chat. But escapes usually mean there's something to escape from. And until that something is resolved, the escape will always be temporary. It's like having an abusive partner and the only relief you get is when they're at work. Sometimes that's what I felt like. An abused partner who has to use makeup to hide the scars. Who has to make up stories to myself and to everyone else to cover up how I really feel.

Except I still don't know how to feel or what I'm feeling. It's so hard to define it. It's like I'm still so mad at Mom, but when I come home, I talk to her like I'm fine. I let her hug me and ask me how school is going. I tell her dorm room stories about drunk girls in the shower at two in the morning. She thinks it's funny when I tell her the campus food makes me sick. But then the other side of me wants to lock myself in a small room and scream until the walls shake. I feel all of those emotions simultaneously.

When I come home on a random evening in late fall, Mom is sitting with a cup of tea, both her legs sideways on the couch with her elbow leaned against the arm but the TV off. She looks like one of those Pop Art images we both like so much. She looks much more serious though, and I immediately sense something's off.

"What's wrong?" I don't even say hi. Mom is someone who doesn't even try to put on a poker face. When something's wrong, you know.

"I was just thinking about some stuff. Come sit with me." Mom slides her legs off the couch and I get right up beside her. "I want to ask you something." I hate when parents do this. "What would you think if Reyna and her son came over for Christmas dinner?"

There it is. Right there in front of me dangling like a chain in a hip-hop video. My initial thought is fuck no. We haven't ever mixed families before, why start now? And I say as much to Mom.

"Why? Why now? We've gone this long without knowing each other, why is it important all of a sudden?"

"Because things are obviously different now," Mom says. "There's really no reason for us to be separated anymore. And I'm not saying we live together as one big happy family, I'm just asking if you're OK with dinner."

"You're asking if I'm OK with meeting my brother. That's a little more complicated than eating organic turkey."

"Yes, I guess that is what I'm asking you. What do you think?"

I'm thinking I should've stayed at school this weekend. And every weekend. Maybe then Mom wouldn't think it's OK to ask me this.

"I think it's a lot to ask. I'm guessing you didn't talk to Jericho about this."

"No, I haven't. I figured I'd see how you felt about it before bringing it up with him."

Mom's philanthropy skills in full swing. She knows how to build support for her cause. And trust me, this is certainly her cause. But as angry as I am that Mom is bringing this up to me right now and as confused as I've been over the past couple of months, there's part of me that just wants to say yes. There's part of me that still looks at Mom and sees someone who needs me to say yes.

She would hate me if she knew what I'm thinking. If she knew that when I look at her, I still see a victim. But how can I not? While Candace's mom was afraid to mount a horse on their ranch in Florida, my mother was skydiving in Vancouver. Dad told me when I was three months old, Mom strapped me on her back for a week of hiking through trails in Colorado. We're talking about a woman who took me and Jericho to Spain for half a summer when we were both barely able to talk.

And she's healed now, I know that. It's what everyone keeps telling me. Even though there's still a hitch in her step, she should be thankful she can walk. And even though she might still slur a word here and there, she should be thankful she can talk. But no one sees what I see, except Mom, of course. She knows what she's lost. That thing that can't be explained, but is as real as these sneakers on my feet. That's the thing that makes it hard for me to say no to Mom. It's the thing that made me tell her the day after she dropped that bomb on us that I understand why she did what she did. Why she kept Reyna a secret for so long.

But that wasn't true. I didn't understand why she kept our birth a secret for so long. I was still trying to make sense of how I felt. I knew I was pissed, or at least, I knew I should be pissed. And the shock of hearing your mother isn't your birth mother hit me like a bad breakup, or so I've heard. No boy has ever broken up with me so I'm going by hearsay on that one. Either way, I was hurt. And I should've stayed hurt a lot longer before letting Mom off the hook.

She was in her bedroom when I crawled up under her duvet and laid down on her shoulder. It was morning, but still dark out. Mom wasn't even awake when I knocked on her door and snuck into her room. But there I was, curled up beside her like a toddler with tears already streaming down my face.

"I love you, Mom." Those were my first words, spoken in between sniffles while Mom hushed me and stroked my hair. "It just doesn't make sense, you know? You're my mother. I know that. You're the only mother I care about, but it just really sucks that I thought I had to keep this secret that wasn't ever a secret. And it messed with me. Thinking Dad had a mistress and not telling you for years really messed with my head."

Mom didn't say anything. She just kept petting me till I finally calmed down and was able to articulate sentences without feeling like I couldn't catch my breath.

"Why did you name me Ever?" That was what I really wanted to ask. It was my first thought when we were sitting in the basement listening to Mom derail everything about my existence. "You said it was because you had a tough pregnancy and didn't want to forget all the pain I gave you because once I was born, it made all the pain worth it. But that's not true. So why did you name me Ever?"

I'm not sure why that was so important to me, but it was. My name means so much. I've never met anyone else named Ever and that makes me feel special. But it's more than that. My name feels mystical. From the moment I started having memories I felt like I've been on a mission to fulfil the purpose of my name. If you actually google the meaning of ever, it means at any time or at all times. That kind of makes sense, but Ever for me means eternal. It means everlasting. It means that whatever I was put on this earth for has to last forever.

So yeah, it's important to know why Mom chose that name for me. And as I was lying there waiting for her to answer, I worried that there wasn't as much thought behind it as I'd like.

"You were impossible, Ever." My mom's morning voice only had a twinge of rasp. She still sounded like she was ready to sing me a lullaby. "After the doctors told me I couldn't have kids, I made myself believe that I didn't want any. The truth is I've always wanted kids. I may not have wanted a husband, but I saw myself living alone with two little girls doing all the incredible things

I was able to do as a child. So when Reyna came into my life and made children possible, and then God gave me a little girl, I promised I'd live my life for that child forever. I named you as a commitment to that promise."

I thought I was done crying, but that launched me back into a fit of tears. Mom and I stayed in her bed for hours, most of the time without words. It was almost noon when we figured some food might be a good idea. Before we made our way downstairs, I picked up the red marker beside the lamp on the side table and wrote Candace on the back of my hand in all caps. We laughed ourselves into tears and stayed in Mom's room another hour.

That morning was the last time we've spoken about Reyna until right now. Now she's asking me if I'm open to expanding our family. Not if there's room, but if I'm willing to offer this estranged part of our family a seat at the table.

I feel uncomfortable trying to think of an answer. I know Mom knows how hard this is for me, but she's not saying anything, which means she wants an answer.

"No." The word comes out and it feels like someone opened a car window on a hot summer day.

"No?" Mom says. I'm not sure what answer she was expecting, but it probably wasn't this one.

"No. I'm not comfortable with them coming here for Christmas or New Years or any other time. I don't wanna deal with that."

Mom listens. She nods her head and doesn't say anything. Maybe I was too abrupt. Maybe I should think it over for a bit. But this is the closest to how I feel. I know because I felt so good saying it.

"I get it," Mom says. She cups my hand in hers and kisses it. "It's a lot to ask. If you change your mind, though, please come talk to me about it." As she's walking away, she tells me that there's some lunch in the kitchen and I should eat. I'm still on the couch wondering if I said the right thing, which is weird for me because I never worry about saying the right thing. But none of this has been normal so I shouldn't be surprised.

"Oh, and your brother went to BC yesterday. He's staying there for the weekend. He actually spoke to me and asked me if I thought it was a good idea. I told him he should go for it."

I was wondering why I hadn't heard from Jericho all day. I've gotten so used to him messaging me that I actually look out for his texts now. But BC? That's a brave move, little Jericho. He's been trying so hard to be tough over the past month, but I guess Candace is still his soft spot. That's one thing he and I have in common. We both can't help ourselves when it comes to Candace. Have I mentioned how special that girl is?

I would normally go up to Jericho's room, but since he's out playing Romeo, I decide to go into the basement instead. It's hard to believe that this is where it all started. A few boys and girls getting together to let out their frustrations. Such a simple thing literally changed my life in a matter of months. I'm not sure if I imagined we'd take it this far when I first thought of it. I was struggling at the time and had a feeling other kids were struggling too. It only made sense to do something about it, or at least try. So I did, and here we are.

If I was texting right now, I'd use the mind blown emoji. Standing in this basement, I can see us all sitting in a circle. I see Mark in his Raptors hat and James with his braids hanging down over his face. Lindsay's observing everyone quietly while Chloe and Trish are playing with each other's hair. Jericho and Candace are giving each other flirty looks. I still can't believe they were a thing. I'm not sure I ever thanked them for what they did. They made this group possible. Little Jericho really stepped up and Candace has always been with me. I'd hate to think of what my life would be like if they weren't in it.

I turn on my Bluetooth and click the Lo-Fi Hip-Hop playlist then sit cross-legged in my usual spot. My phone rings and I already know who it is. I close my eyes.

Kern Carter is a full-time freelance writer and author who has written and self-published two novels — *Thoughts of a Fractured Soul* (novella) and *Beauty Scars*. When Kern isn't penning novels, he curates stories through CRY Magazine, his on-line publication that creates space for artists to navigate through the emotions of their creative journey. He lives in downtown Toronto with his nineteen-year-old daughter.

We acknowledge the sacred land on which Cormorant Books operates. It has been a site of human activity for 15,000 years. This land is the territory of the Huron-Wendat and Petun First Nations, the Seneca, and most recently, the Mississaugas of the Credit River. The territory was the subject of the Dish With One Spoon Wampum Belt Covenant, an agreement between the Iroquois Confederacy and Confederacy of the Ojibway and allied nations to peaceably share and steward the resources around the Great Lakes. Today, the meeting place of Toronto is still home to many Indigenous people from across Turtle Island. We are grateful to have the opportunity to work in the community, on this territory.

We are also mindful of broken covenants and the need to strive to make right with all our relations.